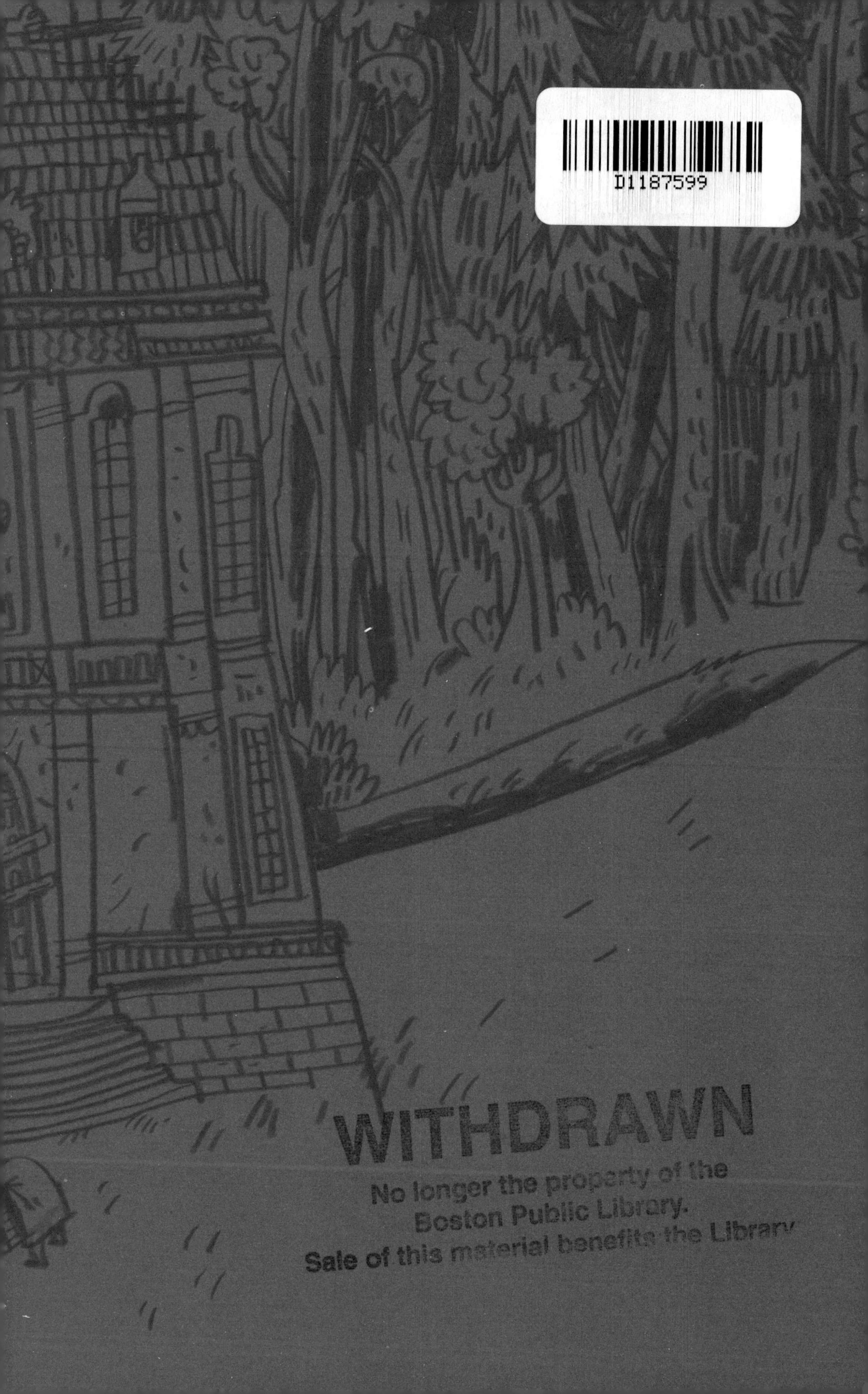

OUR ENCOUNTERS
WITH EVIL:
ADVENTURES OF PROFESSOR J.T. MEINHARDT
AND HIS ASSISTANT MR. KNOX

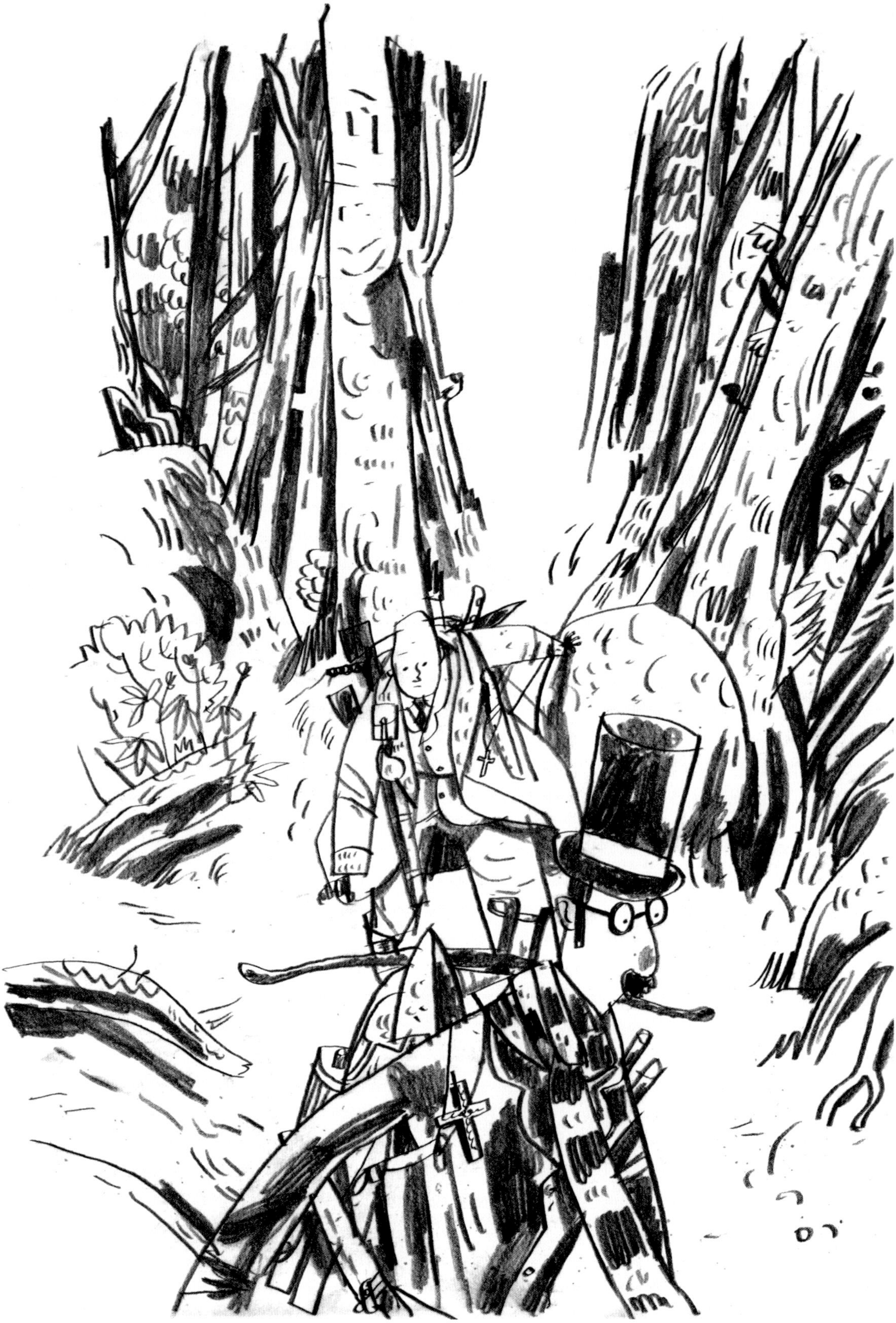

OUR ENCOUNTERS WITH EVIL:

ADVENTURES OF PROFESSOR J.T. MEINHARDT AND HIS ASSISTANT MR. KNOX

Story and art by
WARWICK JOHNSON-CADWELL

Based on characters created by
MIKE MIGNOLA

Letters by
CLEM ROBINS

Cover art by
MIKE MIGNOLA
with **DAVE STEWART**

President and Publisher MIKE RICHARDSON
Editor KATII O'BRIEN
Assistant Editor JENNY BLENK
Collection Designer PATRICK SATTERFIELD
Digital Art Technicians CHRISTIANNE GILLENARDO-GOUDREAU *and* ANN GRAY

DARK HORSE BOOKS

Neil Hankerson *Executive Vice President* Tom Weddle *Chief Financial Officer* Randy Stradley *Vice President of Publishing* Nick McWhorter *Chief Business Development Officer* Dale LaFountain *Chief Information Officer* Matt Parkinson *Vice President of Marketing* Cara Niece *Vice President of Production and Scheduling* Mark Bernardi *Vice President of Book Trade and Digital Sales* Ken Lizzi *General Counsel* Dave Marshall *Editor in Chief* Davey Estrada *Editorial Director* Chris Warner *Senior Books Editor* Cary Grazzini *Director of Specialty Projects* Lia Ribacchi *Art Director* Vanessa Todd-Holmes *Director of Print Purchasing* Matt Dryer *Director of Digital Art and Prepress* Michael Gombos *Senior Director of Licensed Publications* Kari Yadro *Director of Custom Programs* Kari Torson *Director of International Licensing* Sean Brice *Director of Trade Sales*

Published by Dark Horse Books
A division of Dark Horse Comics LLC
10956 SE Main Street
Milwaukie, OR 97222

Advertising Sales (503) 905-2315
Comic Shop Locator Service: comicshoplocator.com

DarkHorse.com

Facebook.com/DarkHorseComics
Twitter.com/DarkHorseComics

First edition: October 2019
ISBN 978-1-50671-166-9
Digital ISBN 978-1-50671-181-2

OUR ENCOUNTERS WITH EVIL

1 3 5 7 9 10 8 6 4 2
Printed in China

Library of Congress Cataloging-in-Publication Data

Names: Mignola, Mike, author, cover artist. | Johnson-Cadwell, Warwick,
  writer, artist, colourist. | Robins, Clem, 1955- letterer. | Stewart,
  Dave, cover artist.
Title: Our encounters with evil : adventures of Professor J.T. Meinhardt and
  his assistant Mr. Knox / story by Mike Mignola and Warwick Johnson-Cadwell
  ; art and colors by Warwick Johnson-Cadwell ; letters by Clem Robins ;
  cover by Mike Mignola with Dave Stewart.
Description: First edition. | Milwaukie, OR : Dark Horse Books, 2019.
Identifiers: LCCN 2019020878 | ISBN 9781506711669 (hardback)
Subjects: LCSH: Graphic novels. | BISAC: COMICS & GRAPHIC NOVELS / Horror. |
  COMICS & GRAPHIC NOVELS / Fantasy. | FICTION / Occult & Supernatural.
Classification: LCC PN6727.M53 O97 2019 | DDC 741.5/973--dc23
LC record available at https://lccn.loc.gov/2019020878

For Warwick, who brought these guys to life.
—MIKE MIGNOLA

*Thanks to Mike for the constant inspiration and
thanks to Katii and Jenny for your patience.*
—WARWICK JOHNSON-CADWELL

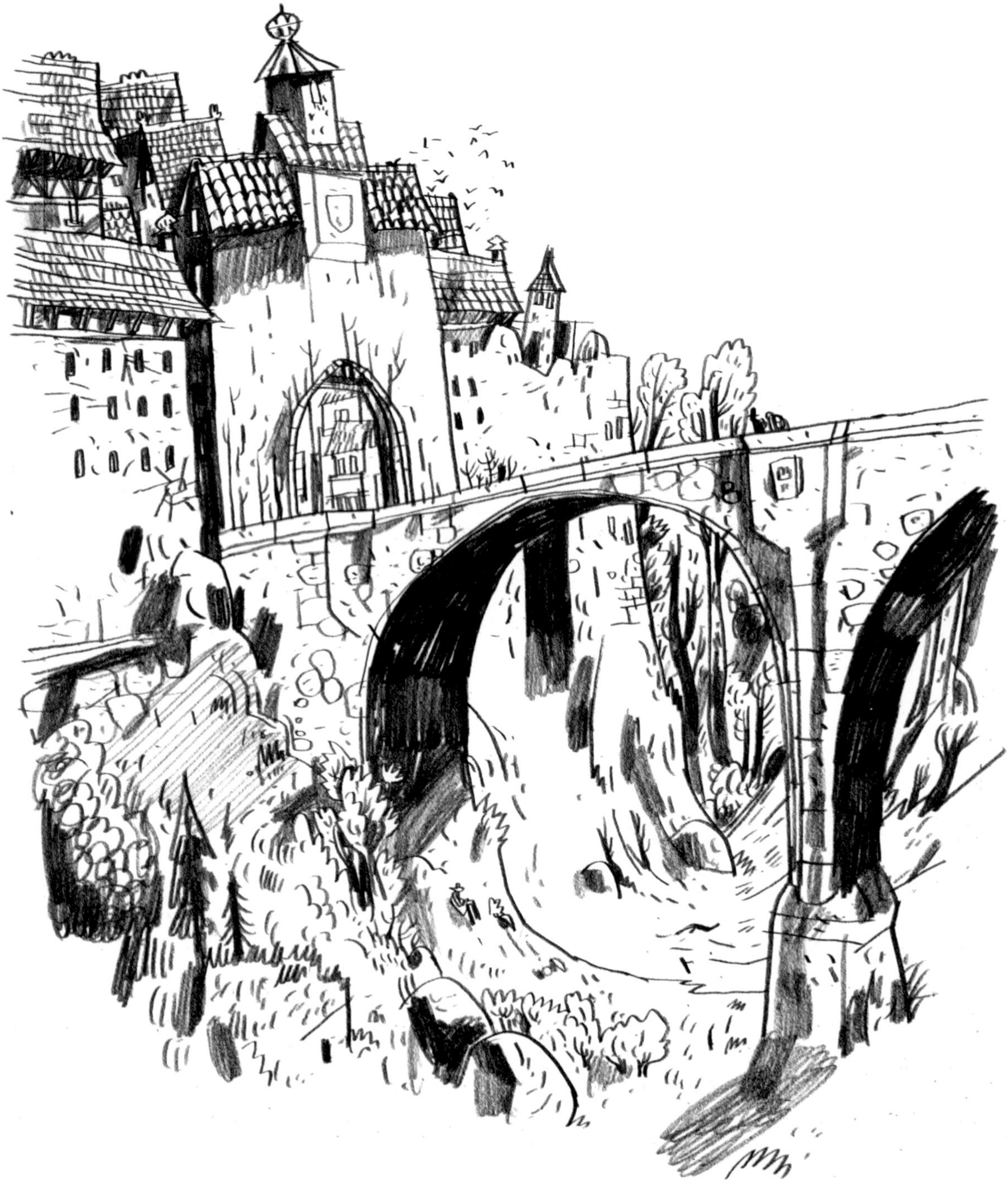

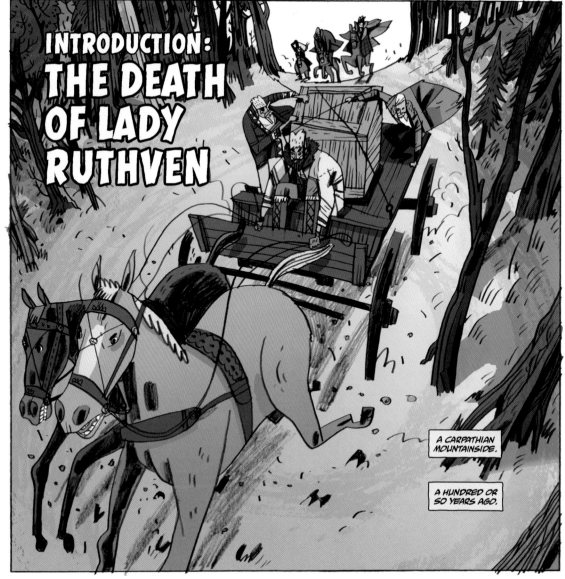

INTRODUCTION:
THE DEATH OF LADY RUTHVEN

A CARPATHIAN MOUNTAINSIDE.

A HUNDRED OR SO YEARS AGO.

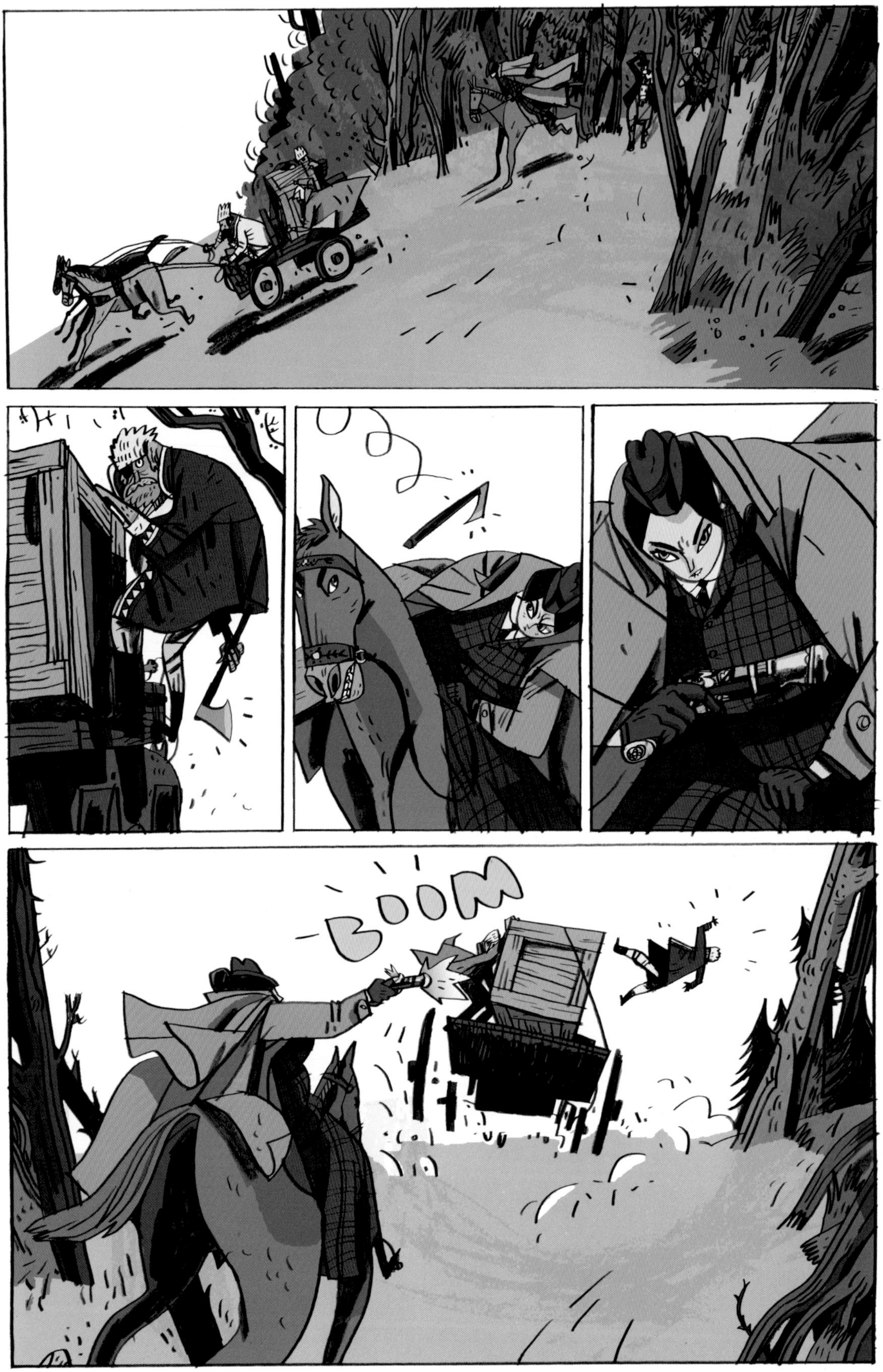
BOOM

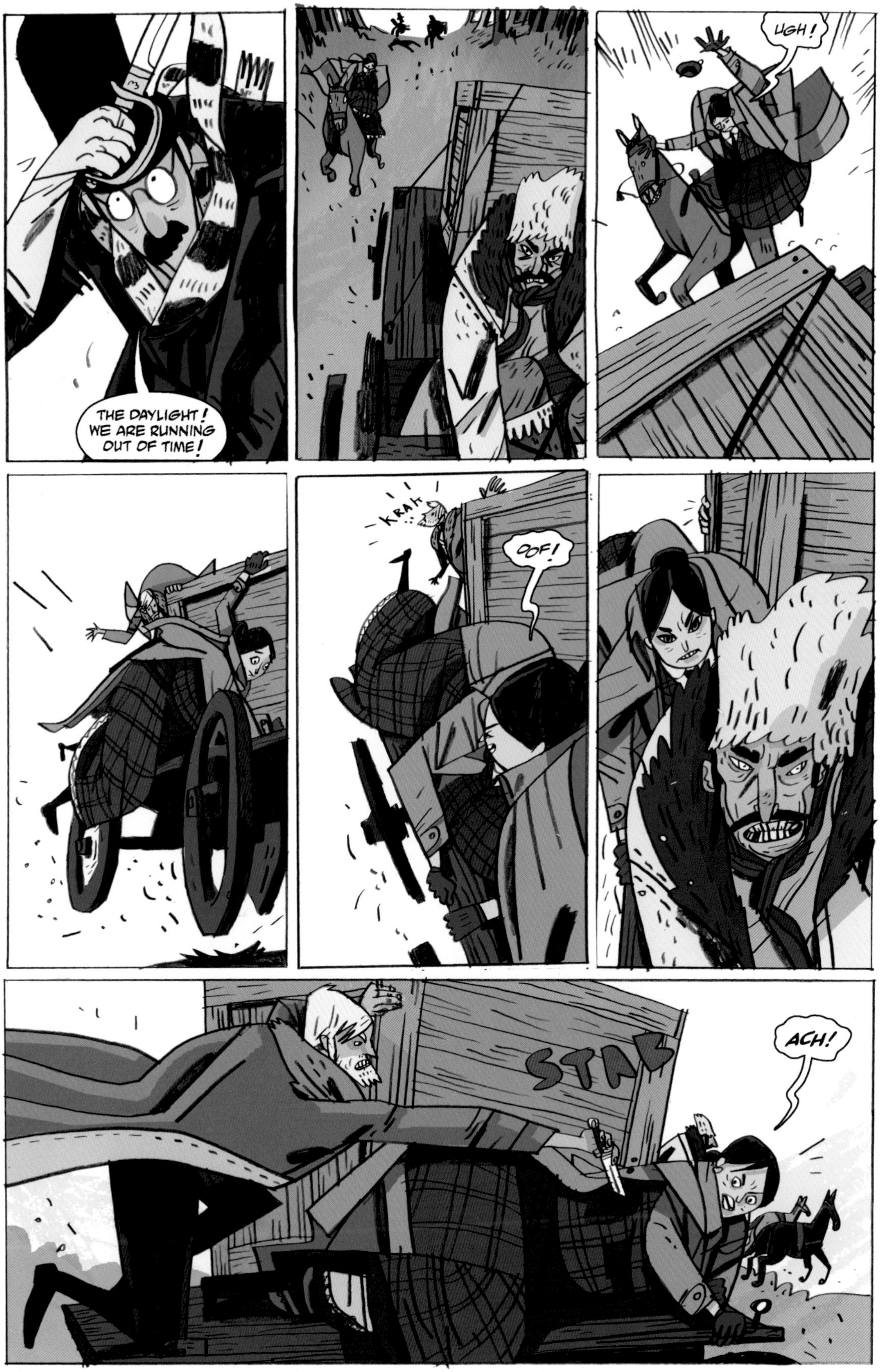
THE DAYLIGHT! WE ARE RUNNING OUT OF TIME!
UGH!
KRAK
OOF!
ACH!

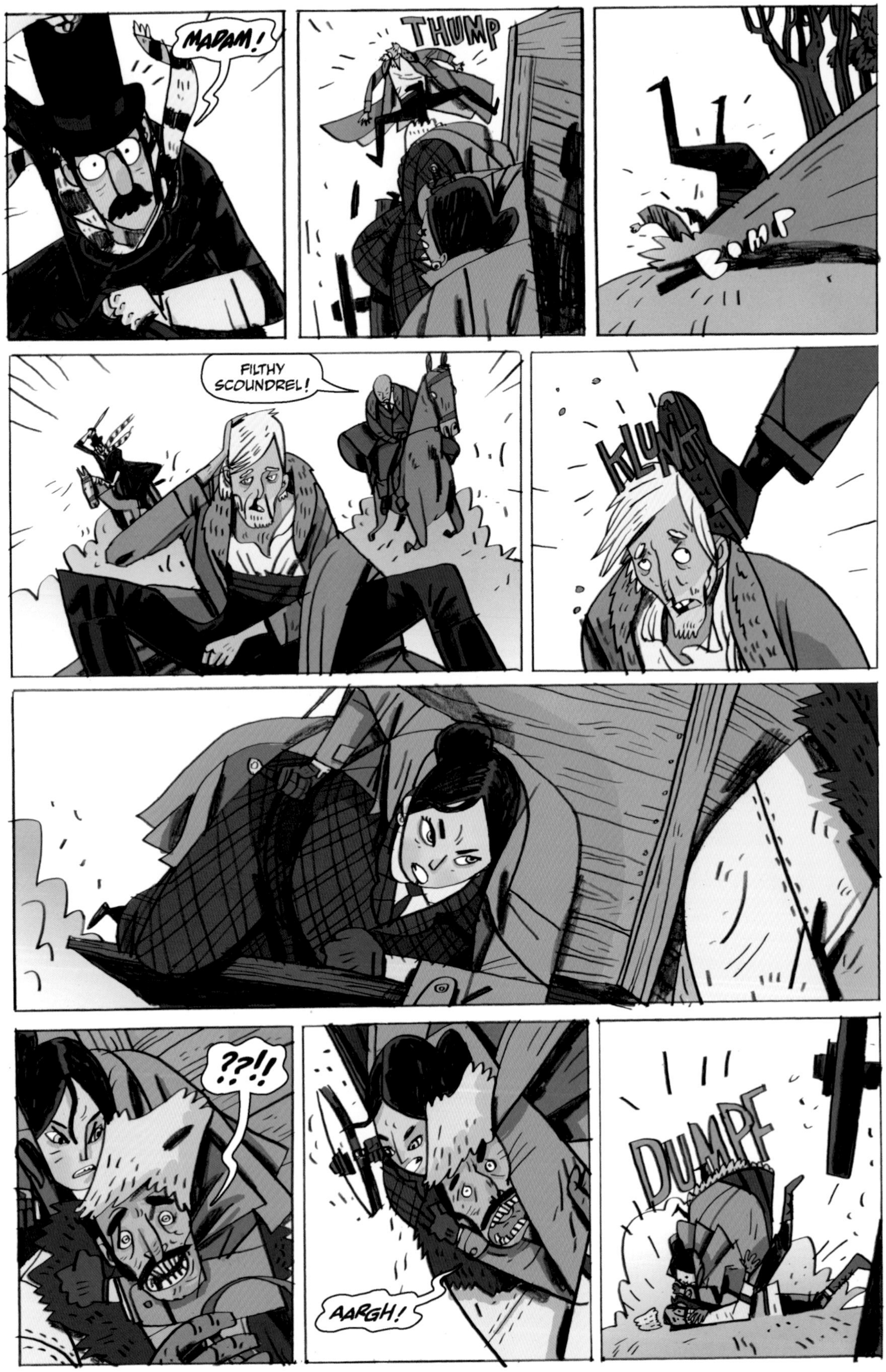
MADAM!
THUMP
BOMP
FILTHY SCOUNDREL!
KLUNK
??!!
AARGH!
DUMPF

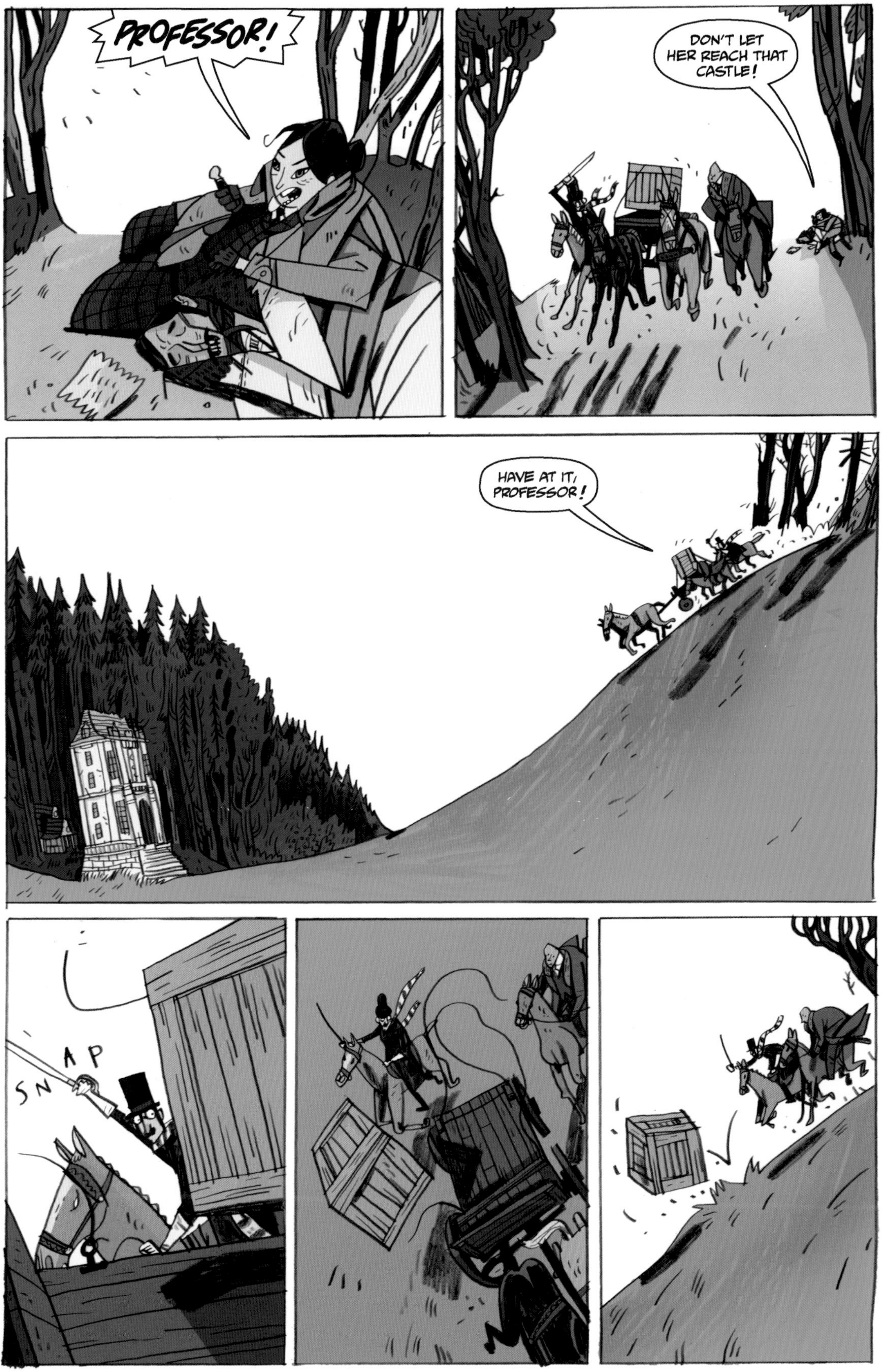
PROFESSOR!
DON'T LET HER REACH THAT CASTLE!
HAVE AT IT, PROFESSOR!
SNAP

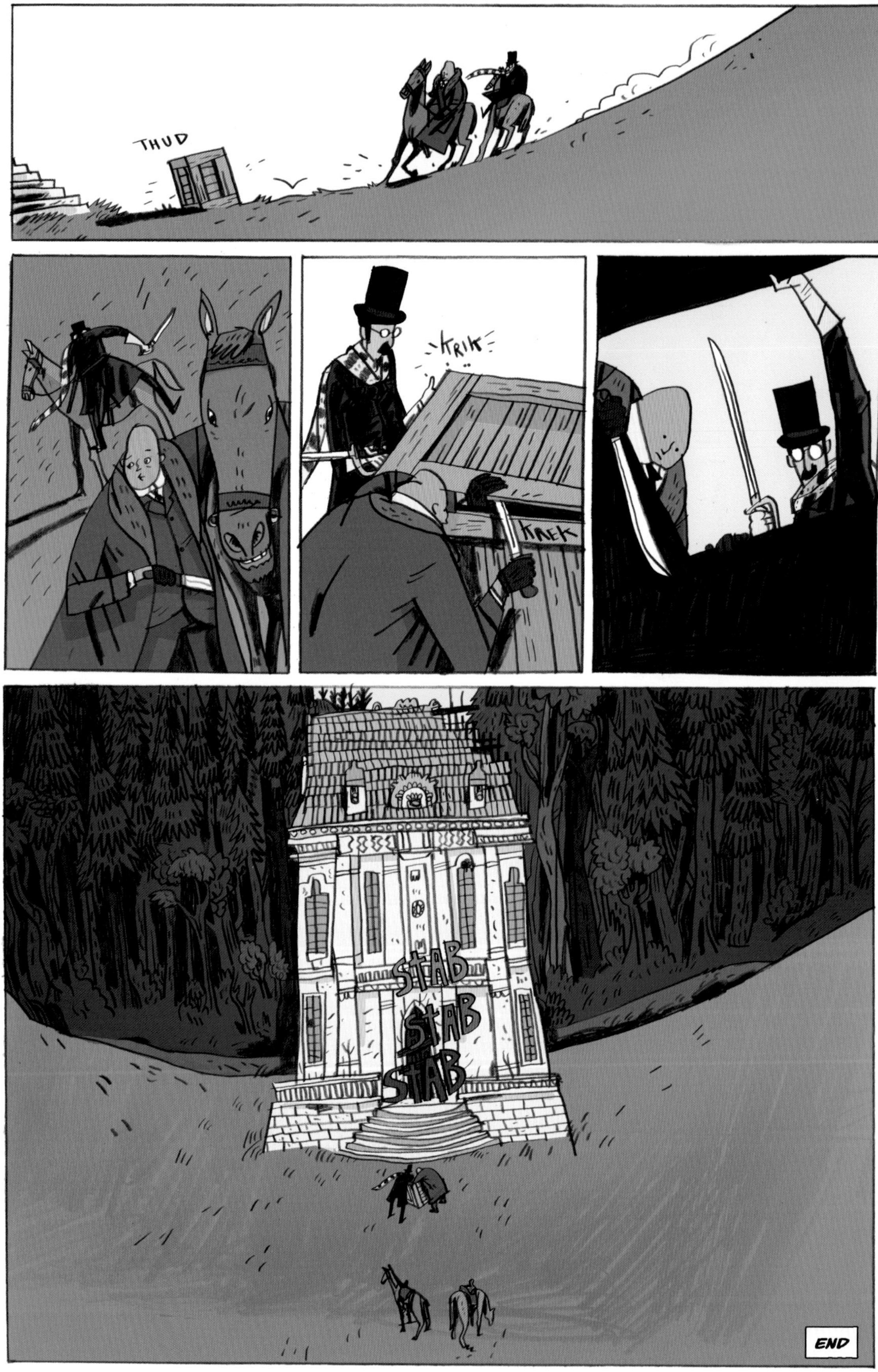
THUD
KRIK
KREK
STAB
STAB
STAB
END

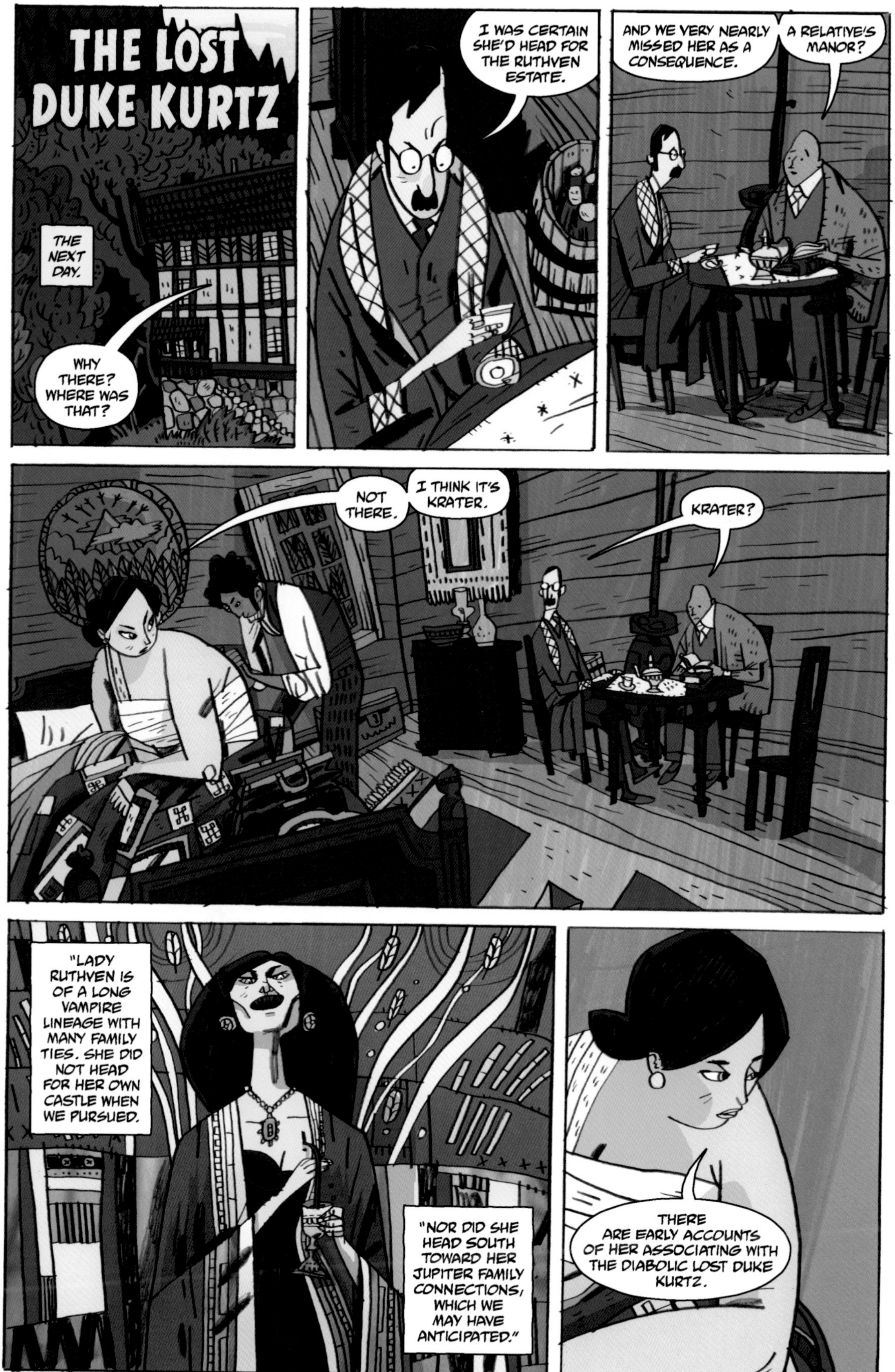
THE LOST DUKE KURTZ
THE NEXT DAY.
WHY THERE? WHERE WAS THAT?
I WAS CERTAIN SHE'D HEAD FOR THE RUTHVEN ESTATE.
AND WE VERY NEARLY MISSED HER AS A CONSEQUENCE.
A RELATIVE'S MANOR?
NOT THERE.
I THINK IT'S KRATER.
KRATER?
"LADY RUTHVEN IS OF A LONG VAMPIRE LINEAGE WITH MANY FAMILY TIES. SHE DID NOT HEAD FOR HER OWN CASTLE WHEN WE PURSUED.
"NOR DID SHE HEAD SOUTH TOWARD HER JUPITER FAMILY CONNECTIONS, WHICH WE MAY HAVE ANTICIPATED."
THERE ARE EARLY ACCOUNTS OF HER ASSOCIATING WITH THE DIABOLIC LOST DUKE KURTZ.

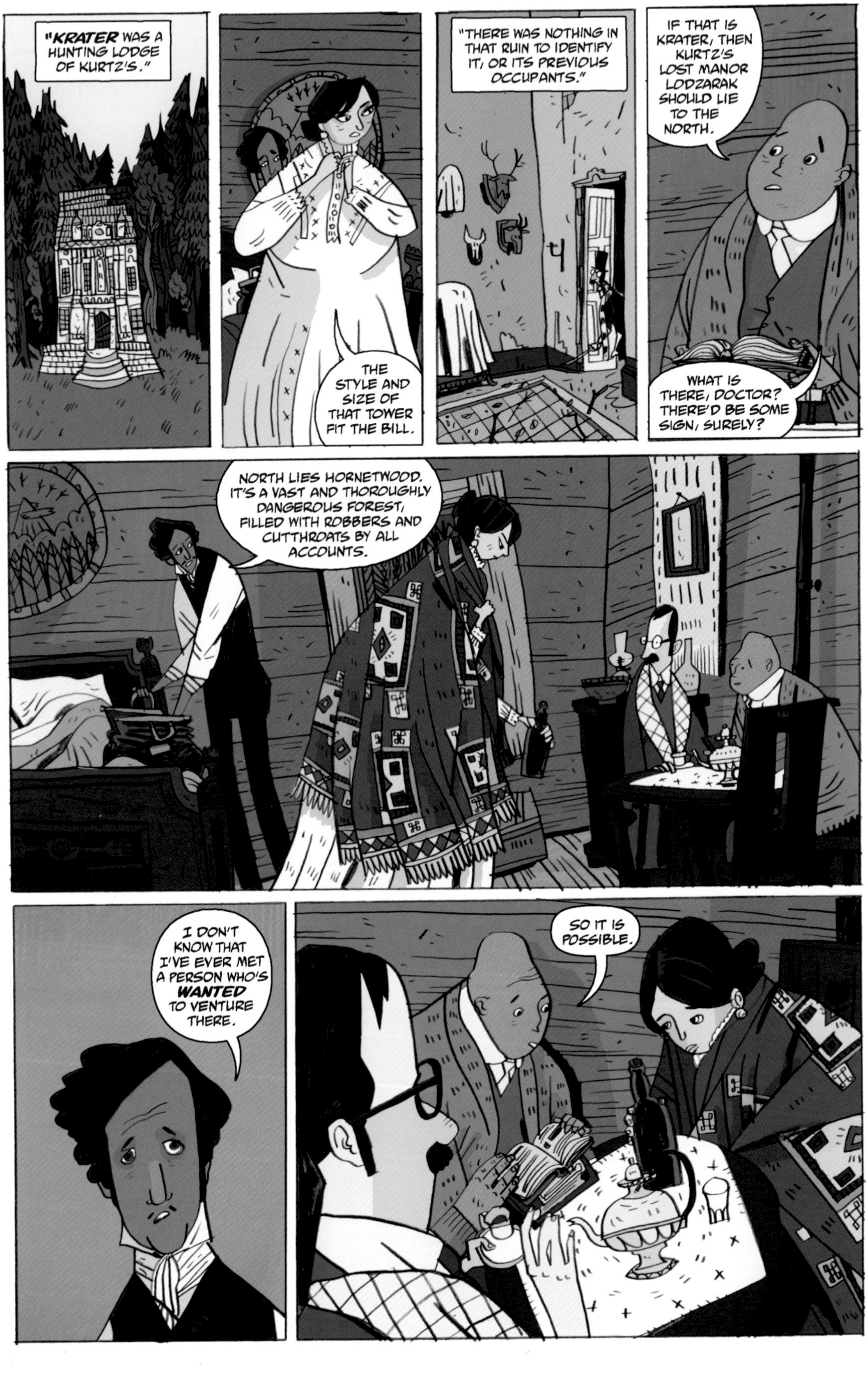
"KRATER WAS A HUNTING LODGE OF KURTZ'S."
THE STYLE AND SIZE OF THAT TOWER FIT THE BILL.
"THERE WAS NOTHING IN THAT RUIN TO IDENTIFY IT, OR ITS PREVIOUS OCCUPANTS."
IF THAT IS KRATER, THEN KURTZ'S LOST MANOR LODZARAK SHOULD LIE TO THE NORTH.
WHAT IS THERE, DOCTOR? THERE'D BE SOME SIGN, SURELY?
NORTH LIES HORNETWOOD. IT'S A VAST AND THOROUGHLY DANGEROUS FOREST, FILLED WITH ROBBERS AND CUTTHROATS BY ALL ACCOUNTS.
I DON'T KNOW THAT I'VE EVER MET A PERSON WHO'S WANTED TO VENTURE THERE.
SO IT IS POSSIBLE.

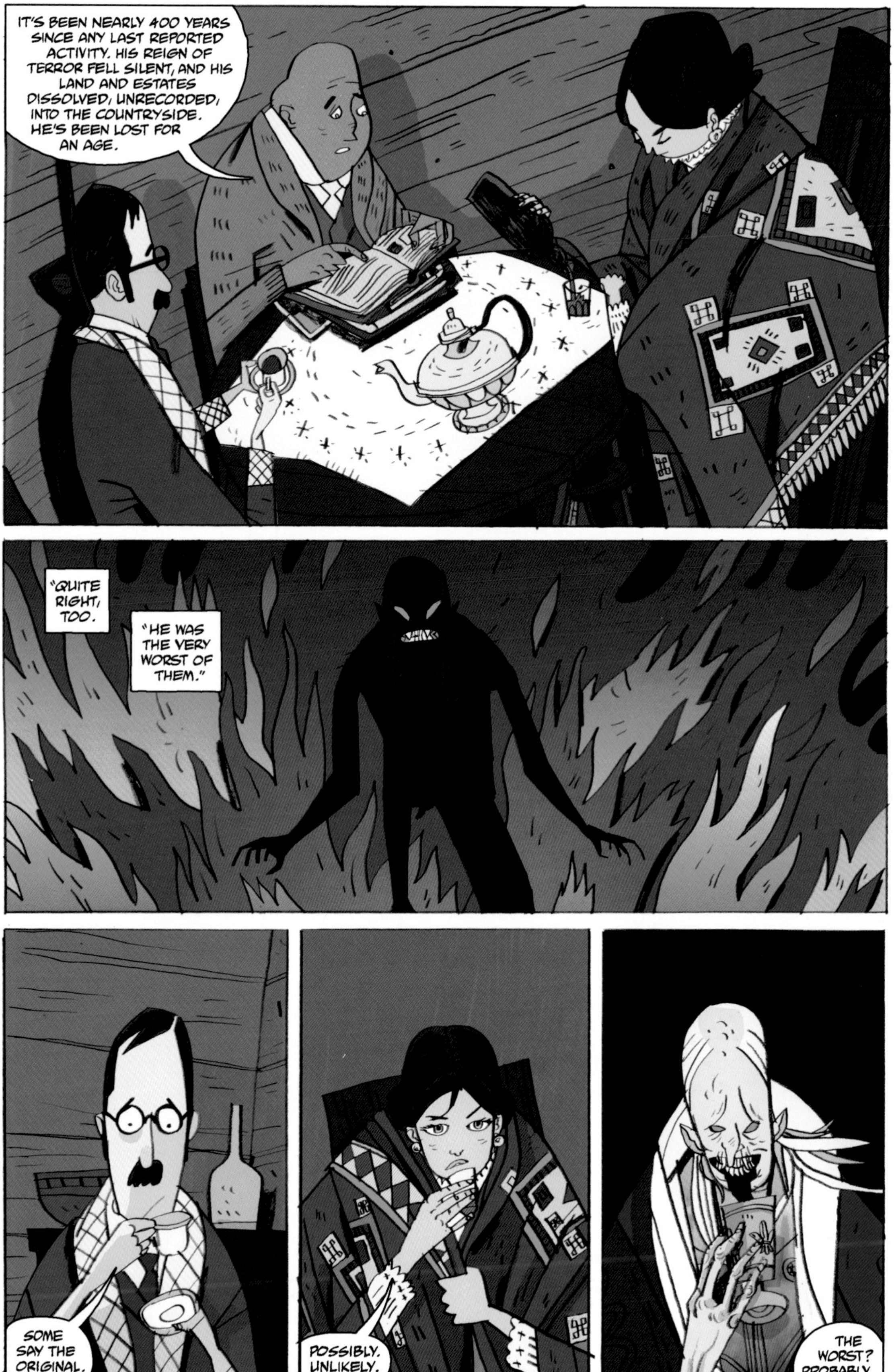
IT'S BEEN NEARLY 400 YEARS SINCE ANY LAST REPORTED ACTIVITY. HIS REIGN OF TERROR FELL SILENT, AND HIS LAND AND ESTATES DISSOLVED, UNRECORDED, INTO THE COUNTRYSIDE. HE'S BEEN LOST FOR AN AGE.
"QUITE RIGHT, TOO.
"HE WAS THE VERY WORST OF THEM."
SOME SAY THE ORIGINAL.
POSSIBLY. UNLIKELY.
THE WORST? PROBABLY.

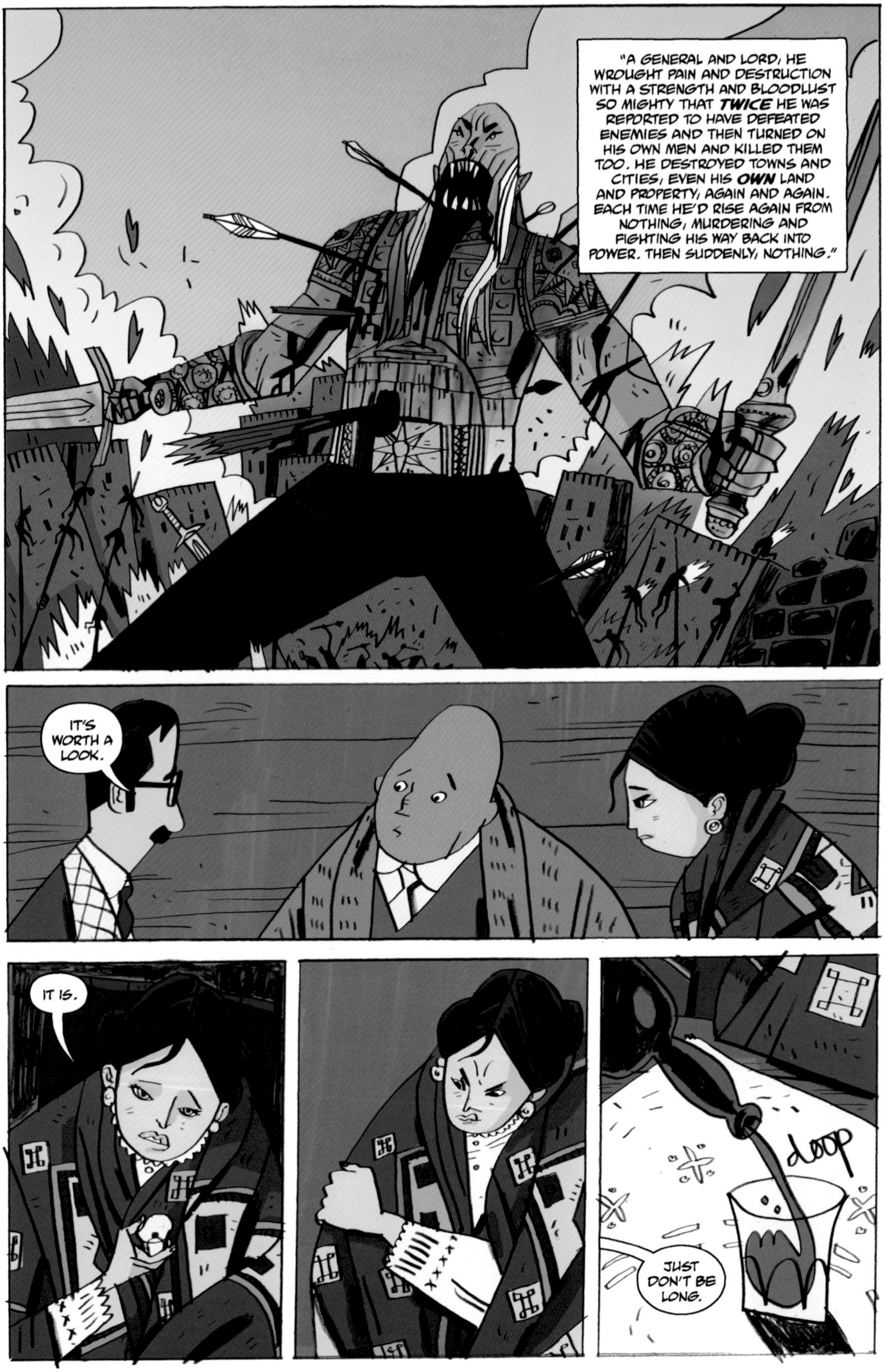
"A GENERAL AND LORD, HE WROUGHT PAIN AND DESTRUCTION WITH A STRENGTH AND BLOODLUST SO MIGHTY THAT TWICE HE WAS REPORTED TO HAVE DEFEATED ENEMIES AND THEN TURNED ON HIS OWN MEN AND KILLED THEM TOO. HE DESTROYED TOWNS AND CITIES, EVEN HIS OWN LAND AND PROPERTY, AGAIN AND AGAIN. EACH TIME HE'D RISE AGAIN FROM NOTHING, MURDERING AND FIGHTING HIS WAY BACK INTO POWER. THEN SUDDENLY, NOTHING."
IT'S WORTH A LOOK.
IT IS.
bloop
JUST DON'T BE LONG.

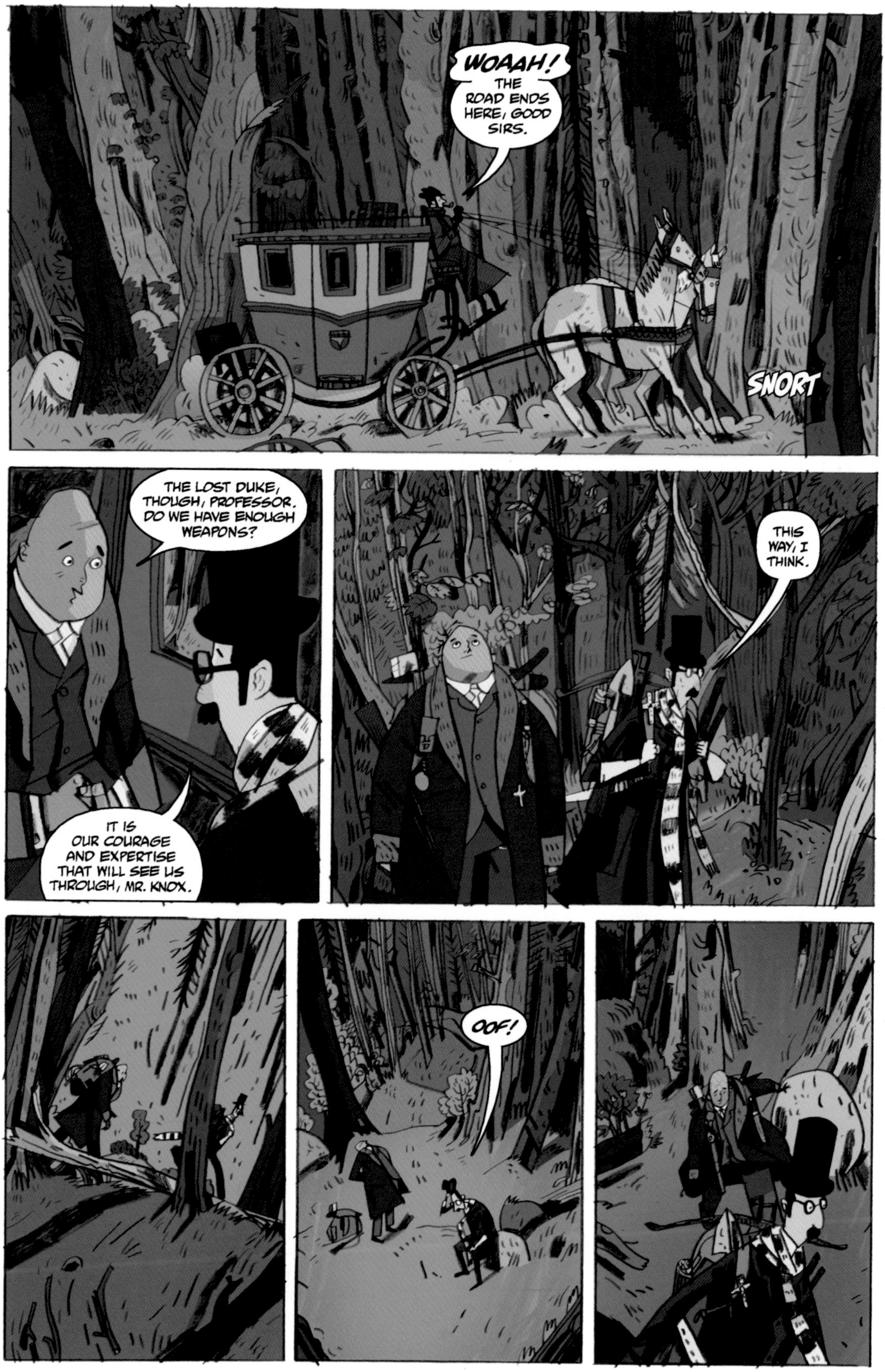
WOAAH! THE ROAD ENDS HERE, GOOD SIRS.
SNORT
THE LOST DUKE, THOUGH, PROFESSOR. DO WE HAVE ENOUGH WEAPONS?
IT IS OUR COURAGE AND EXPERTISE THAT WILL SEE US THROUGH, MR. KNOX.
THIS WAY, I THINK.
OOF!

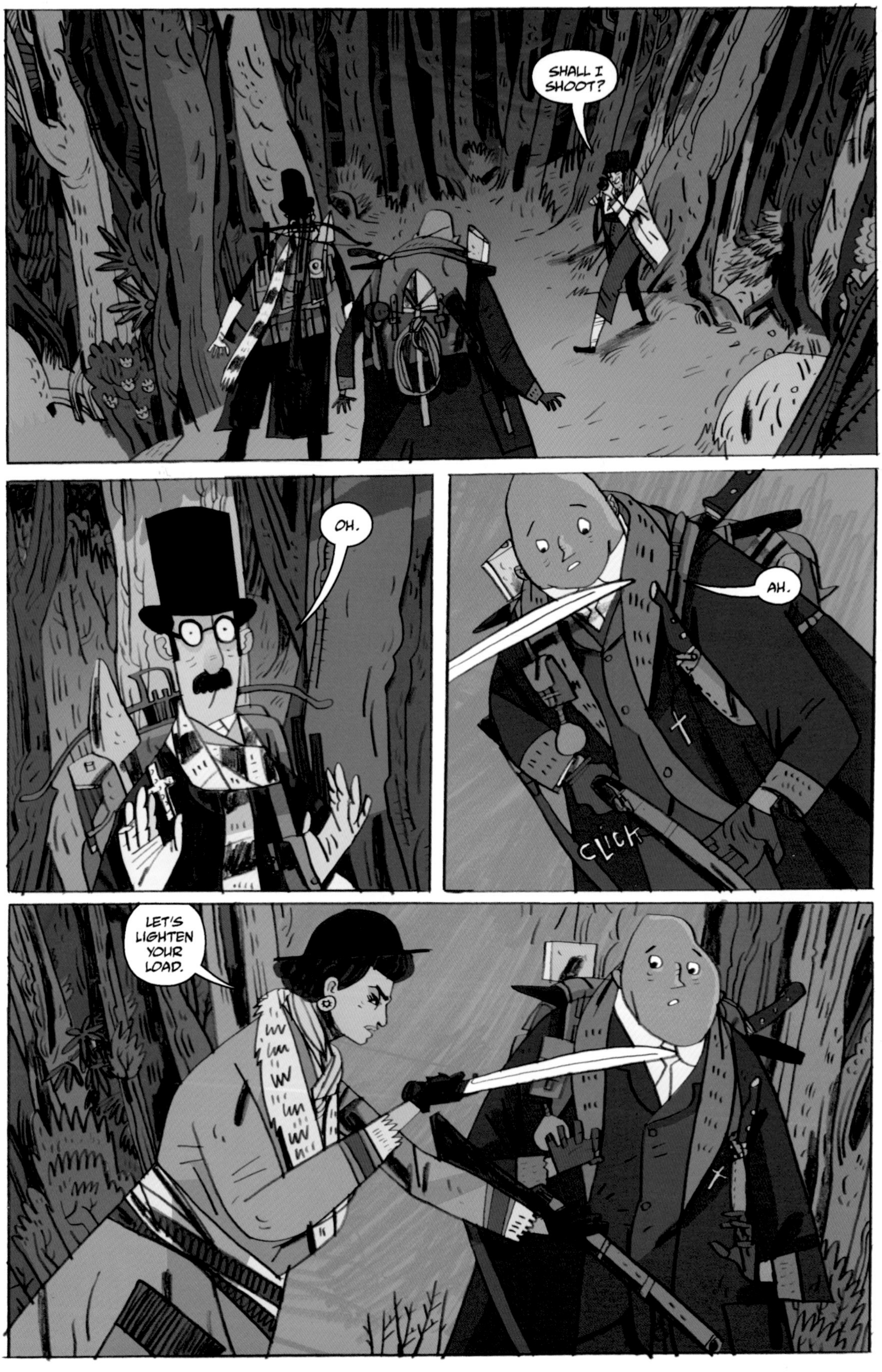
SHALL I SHOOT?
OH.
AH.
CLICK
LET'S LIGHTEN YOUR LOAD.

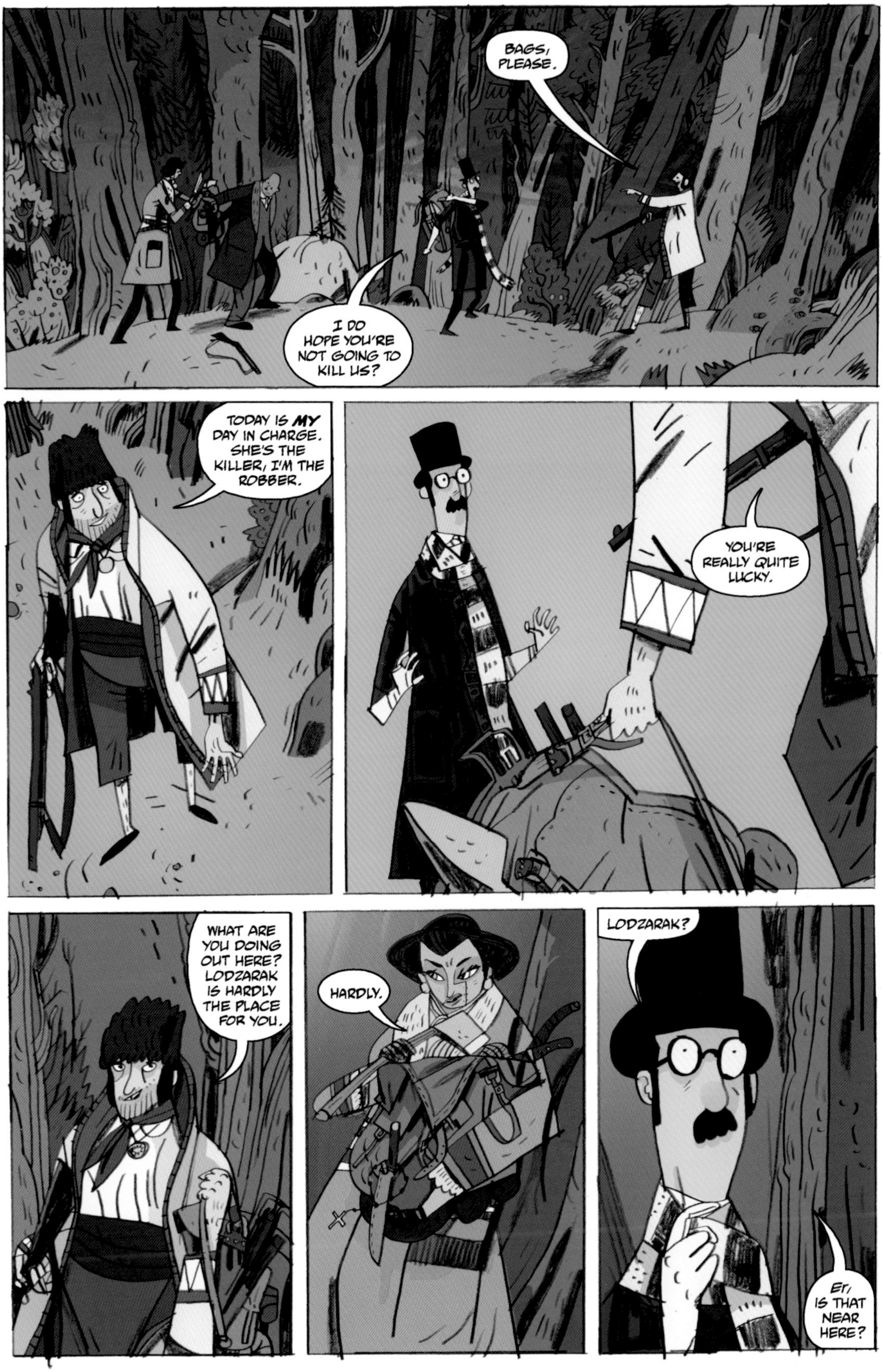
BAGS, PLEASE.
I DO HOPE YOU'RE NOT GOING TO KILL US?
TODAY IS MY DAY IN CHARGE. SHE'S THE KILLER, I'M THE ROBBER.
YOU'RE REALLY QUITE LUCKY.
WHAT ARE YOU DOING OUT HERE? LODZARAK IS HARDLY THE PLACE FOR YOU.
HARDLY.
LODZARAK?
Er, IS THAT NEAR HERE?

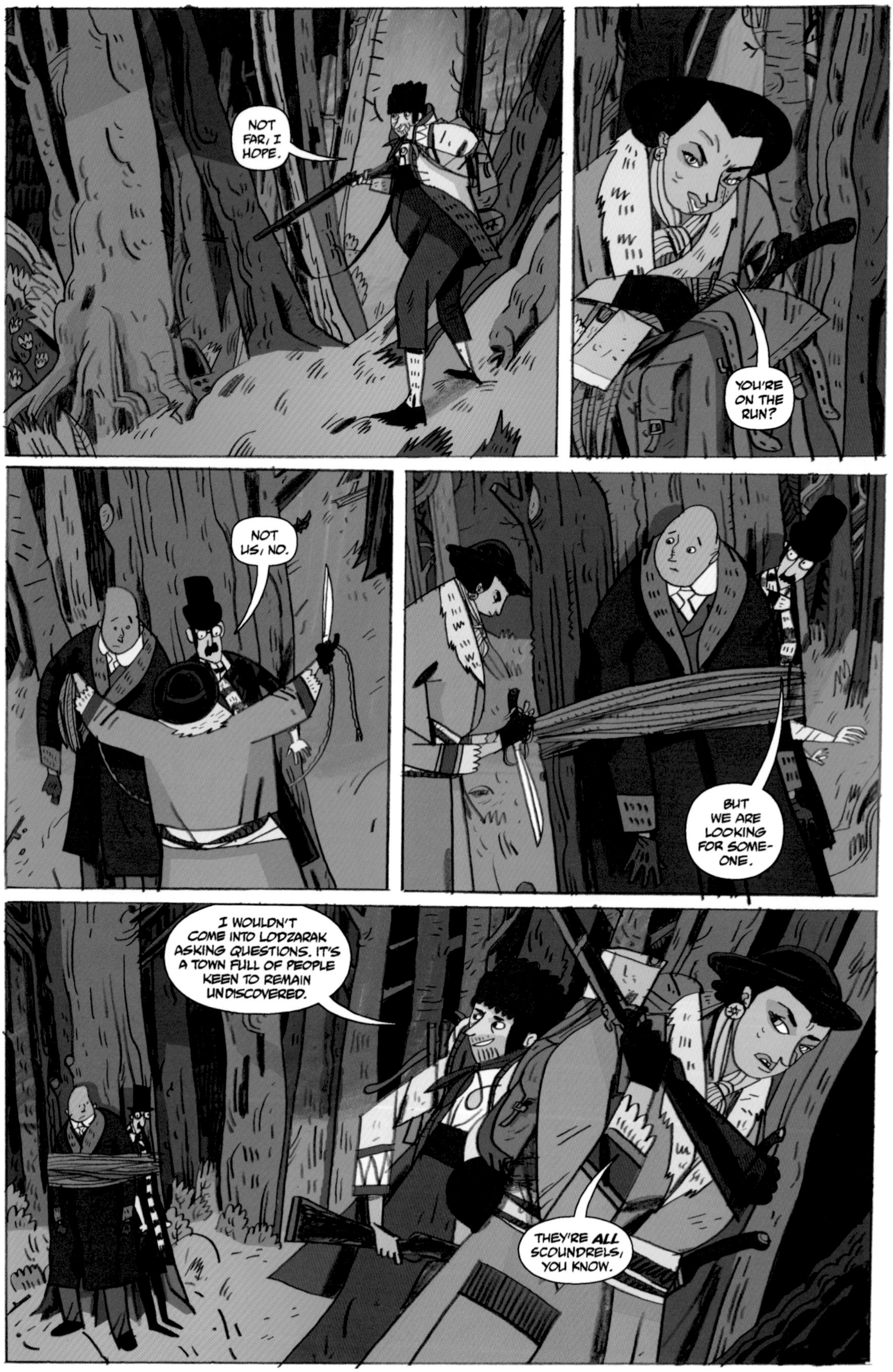
NOT FAR, I HOPE.
YOU'RE ON THE RUN?
NOT US, NO.
BUT WE ARE LOOKING FOR SOME-ONE.
I WOULDN'T COME INTO LODZARAK ASKING QUESTIONS. IT'S A TOWN FULL OF PEOPLE KEEN TO REMAIN UNDISCOVERED.
THEY'RE ALL SCOUNDRELS, YOU KNOW.

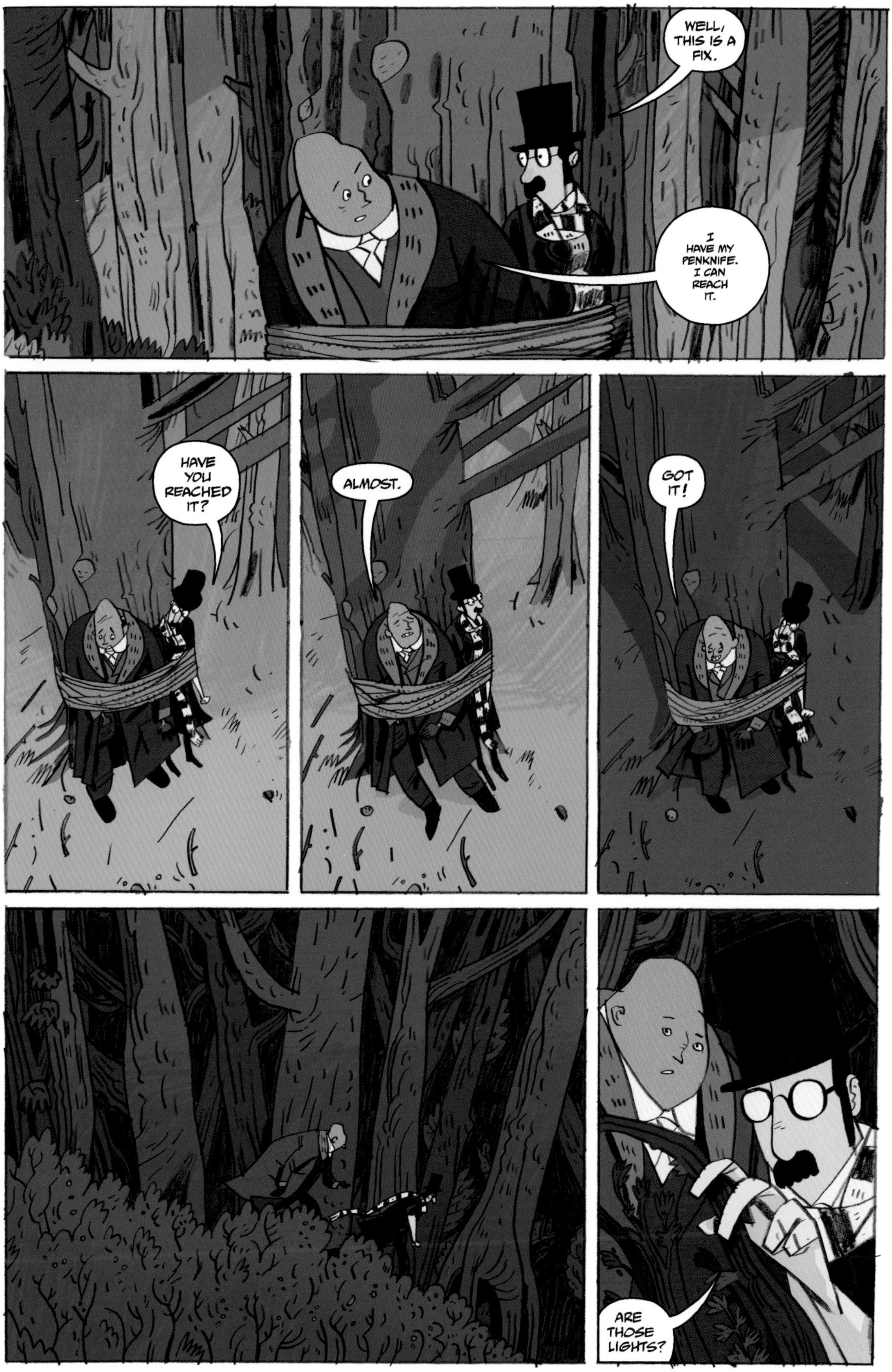
WELL, THIS IS A FIX.
I HAVE MY PENKNIFE. I CAN REACH IT.
HAVE YOU REACHED IT?
ALMOST.
GOT IT!
ARE THOSE LIGHTS?

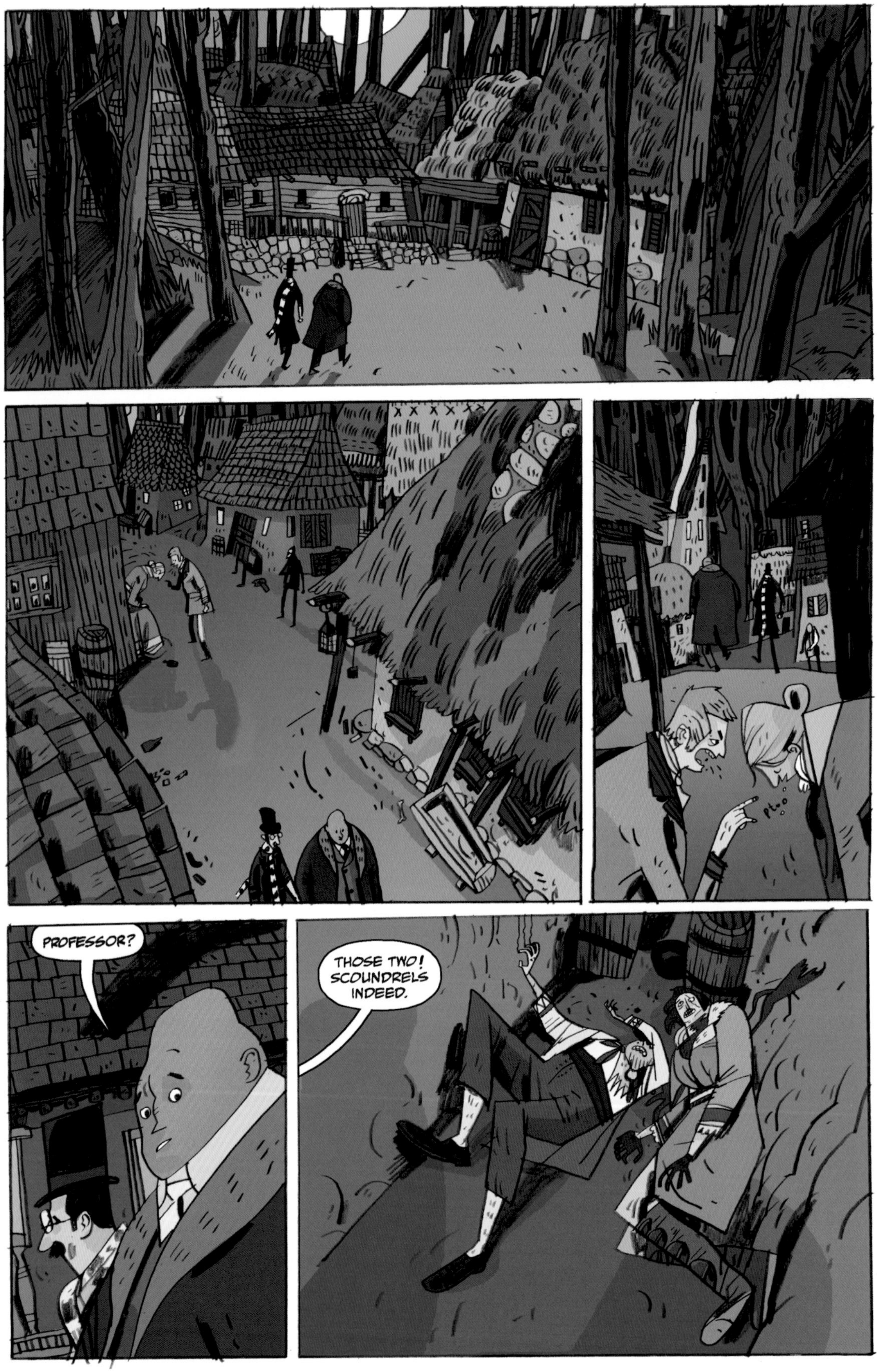
PROFESSOR?
THOSE TWO! SCOUNDRELS INDEED.

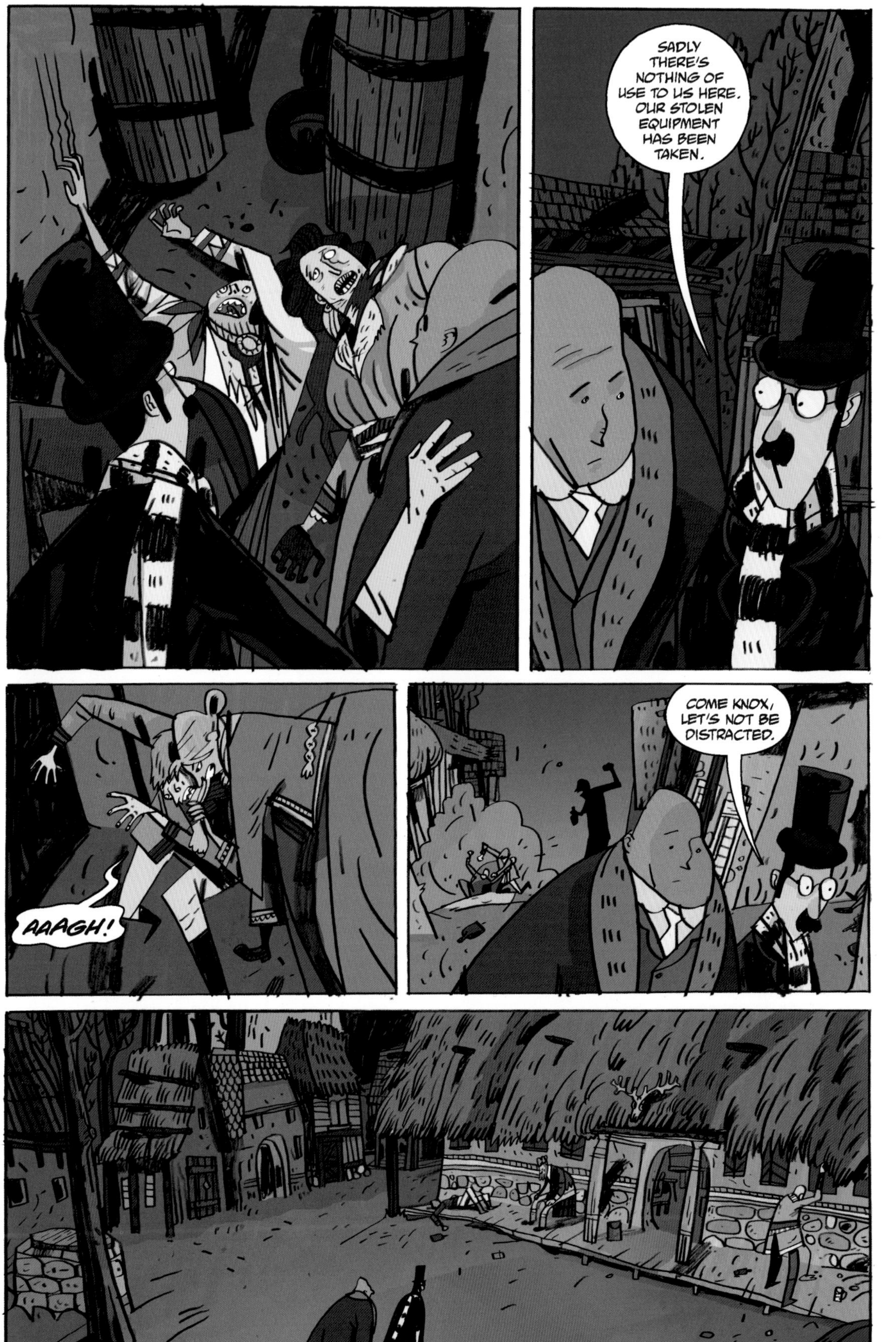
SADLY THERE'S NOTHING OF USE TO US HERE. OUR STOLEN EQUIPMENT HAS BEEN TAKEN.
AAAGH!
COME KNOX, LET'S NOT BE DISTRACTED.

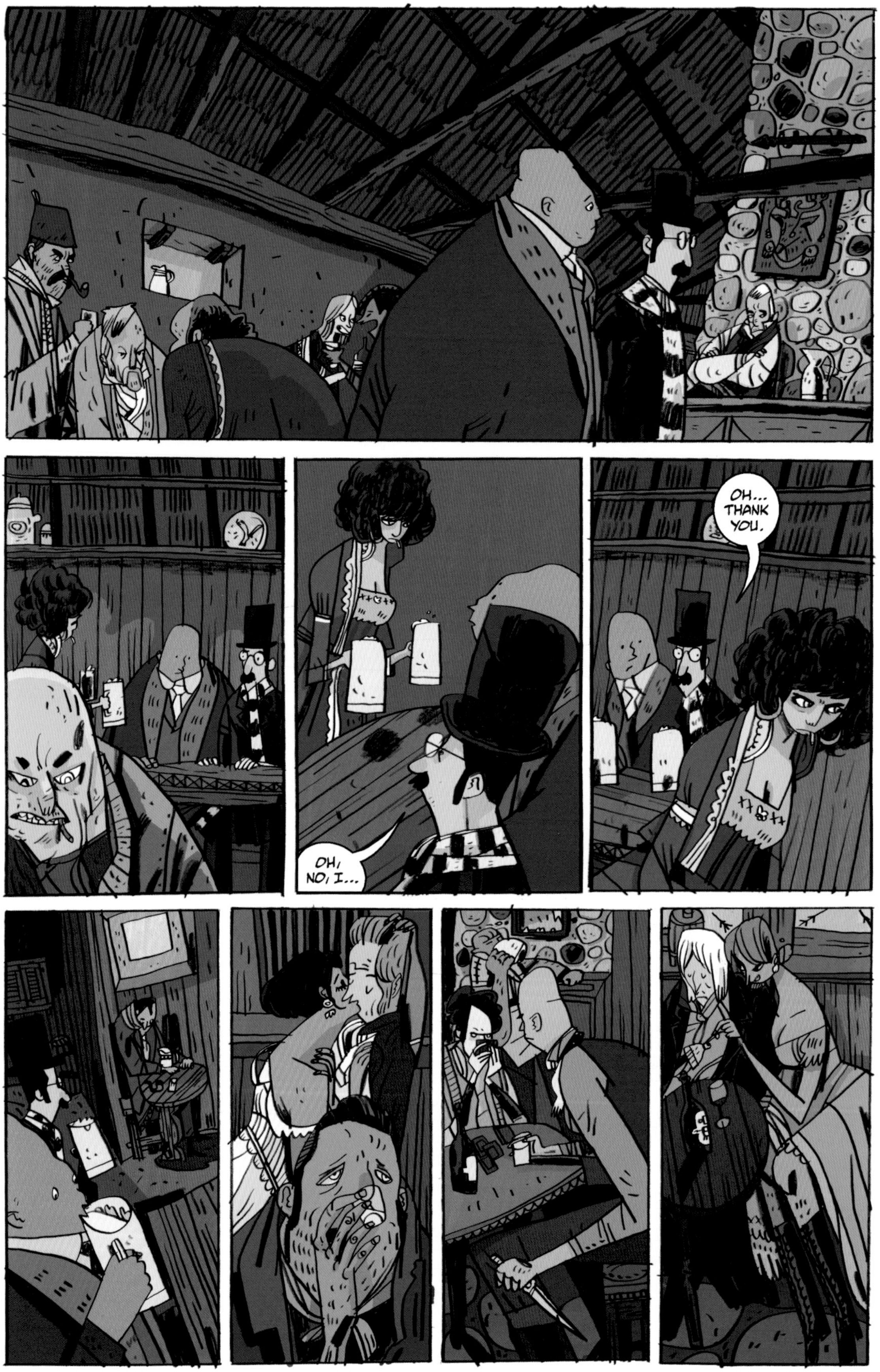
OH, NO, I...
OH... THANK YOU.

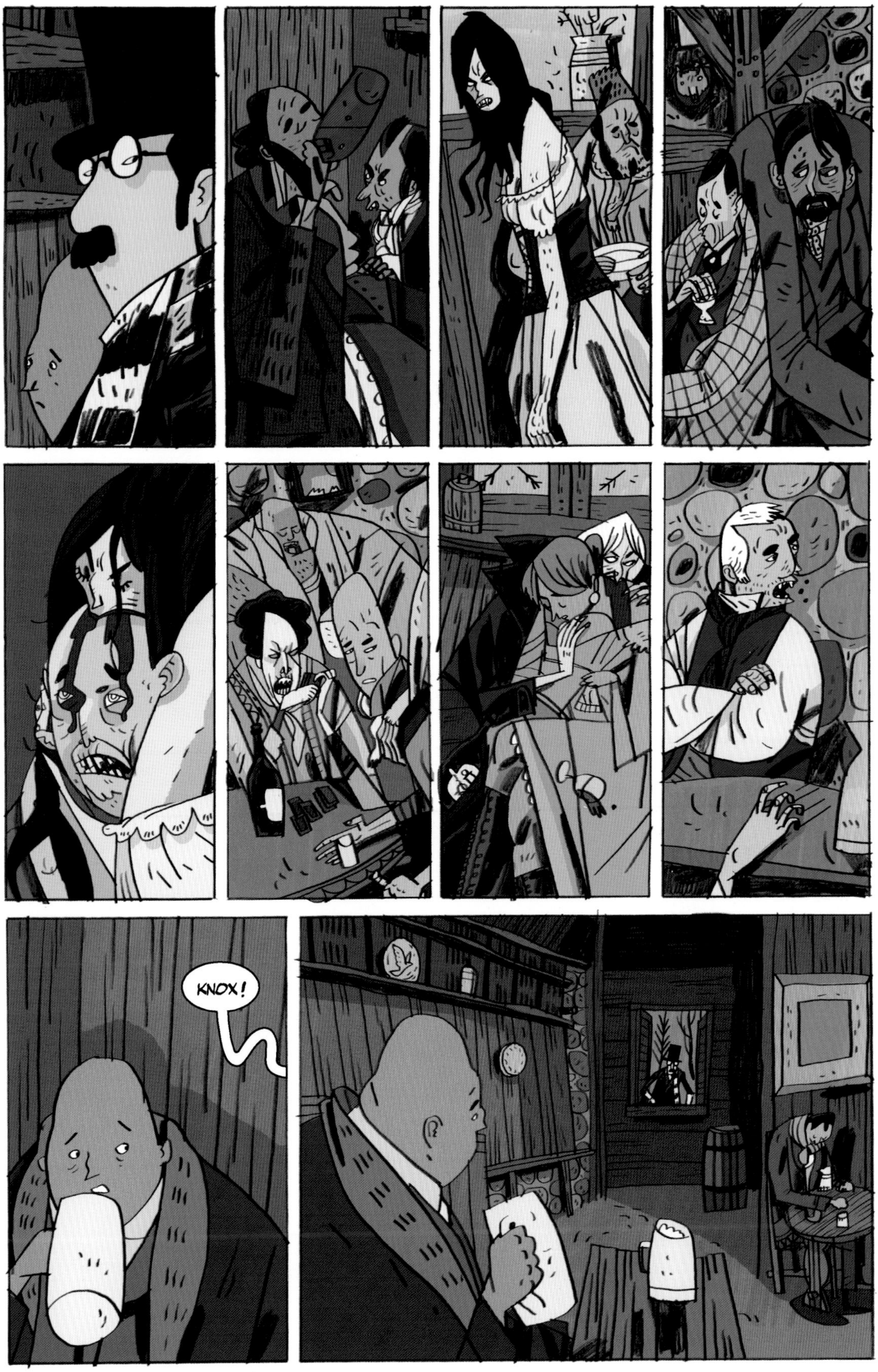
KNOX!

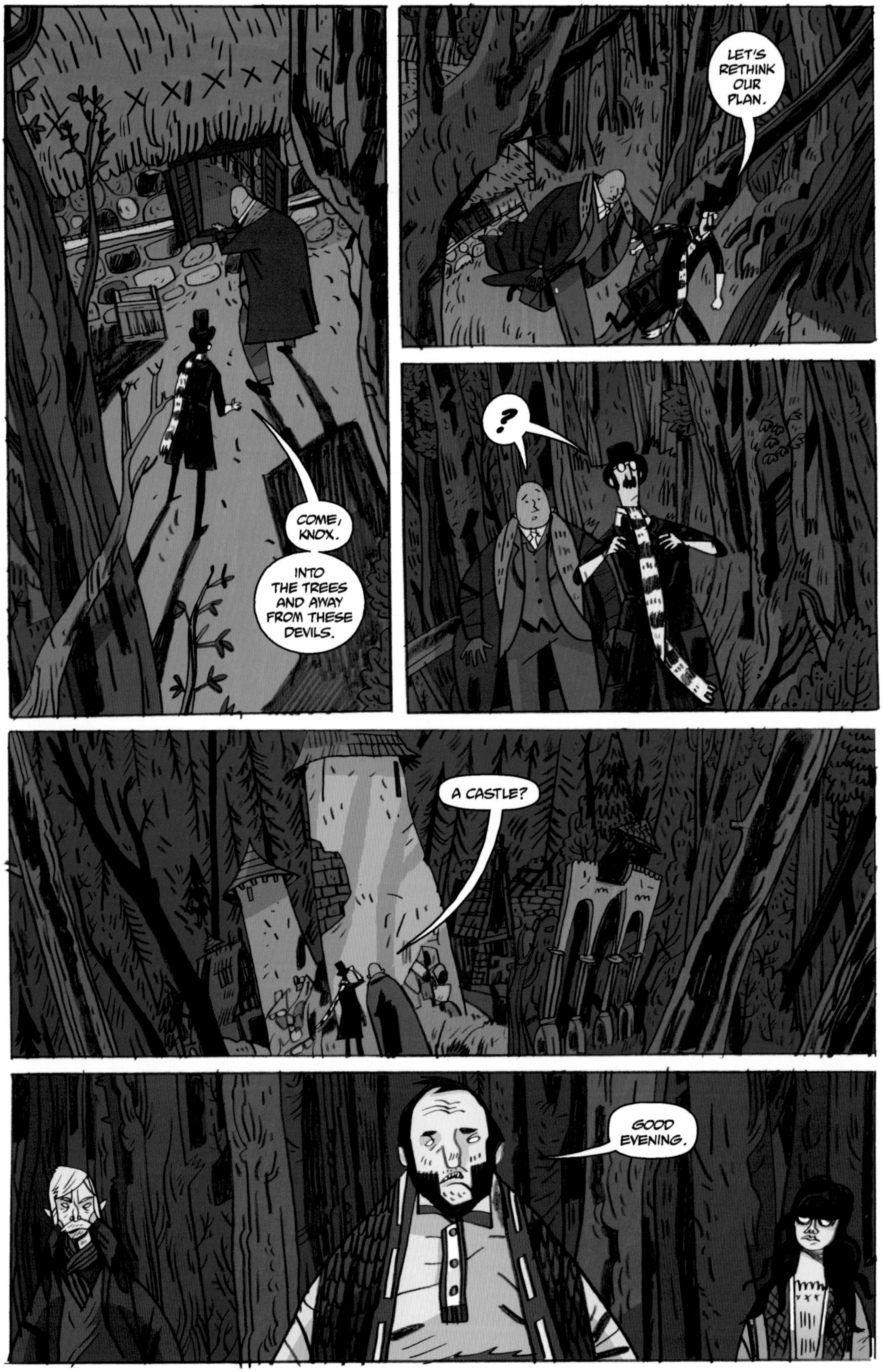
COME, KNOX.
INTO THE TREES AND AWAY FROM THESE DEVILS.
LET'S RETHINK OUR PLAN.
?
A CASTLE?
GOOD EVENING.

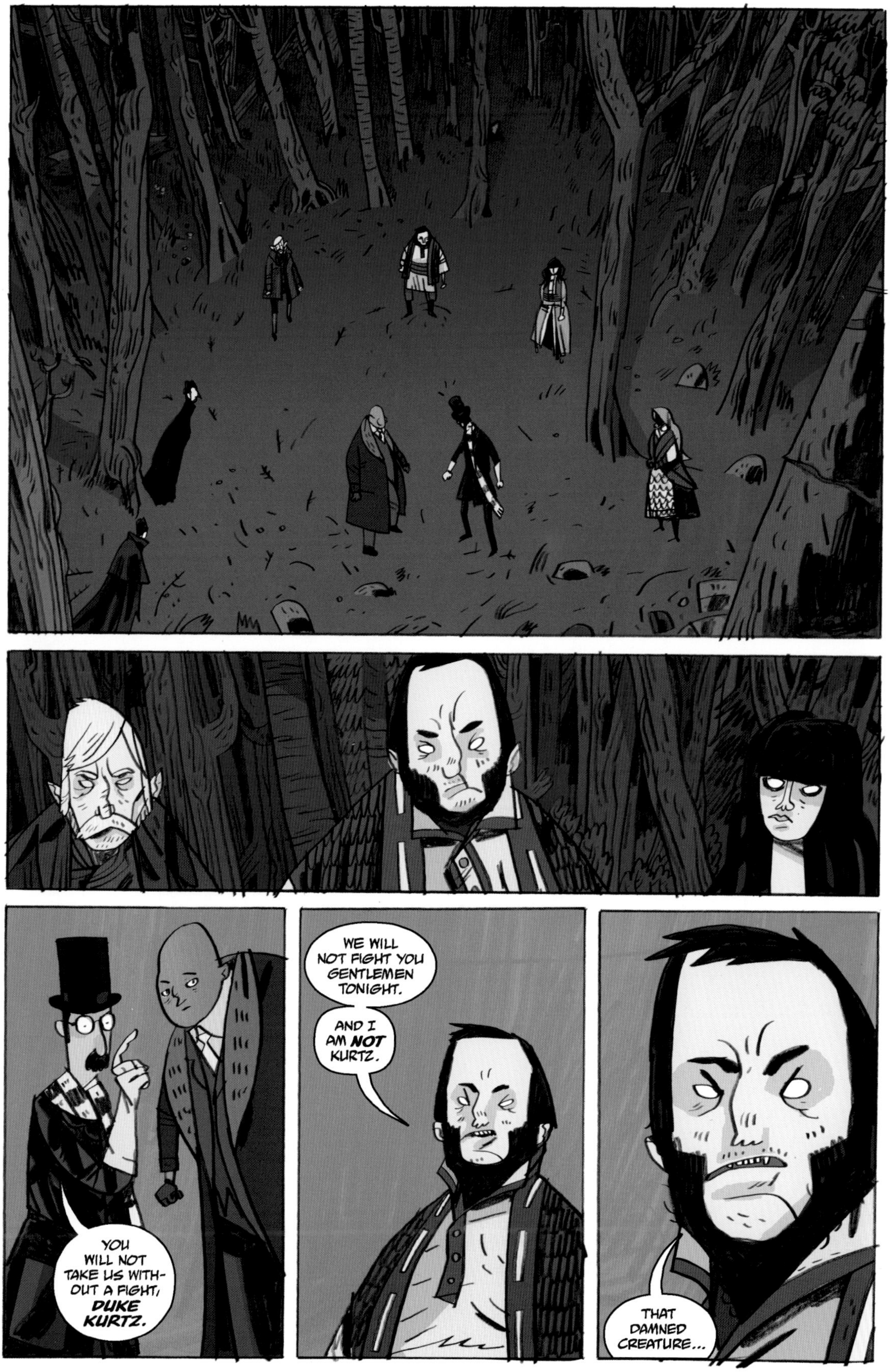
YOU WILL NOT TAKE US WITH- OUT A FIGHT, DUKE KURTZ.
WE WILL NOT FIGHT YOU GENTLEMEN TONIGHT.
AND I AM NOT KURTZ.
THAT DAMNED CREATURE...

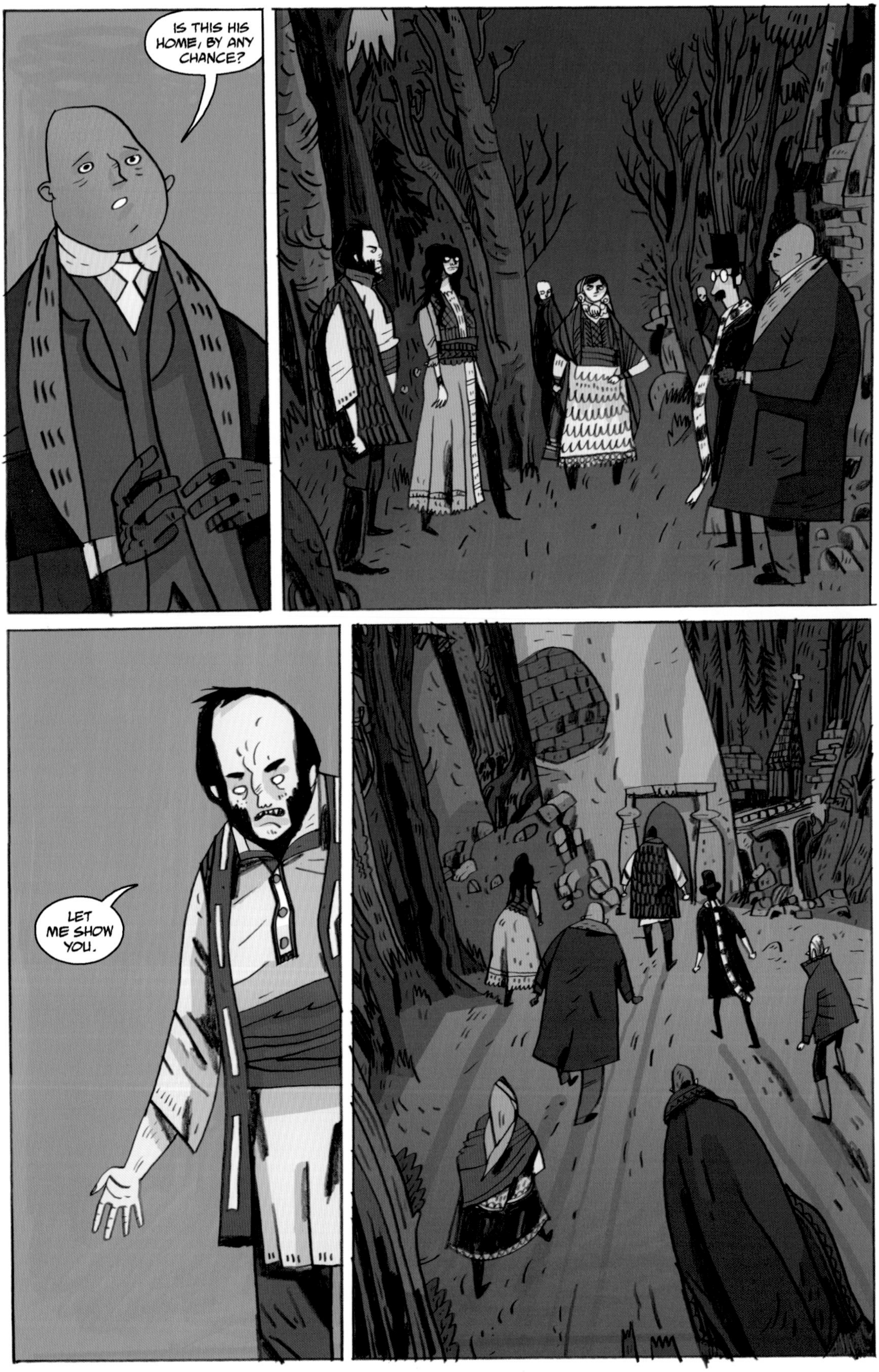
IS THIS HIS HOME, BY ANY CHANCE?
LET ME SHOW YOU.

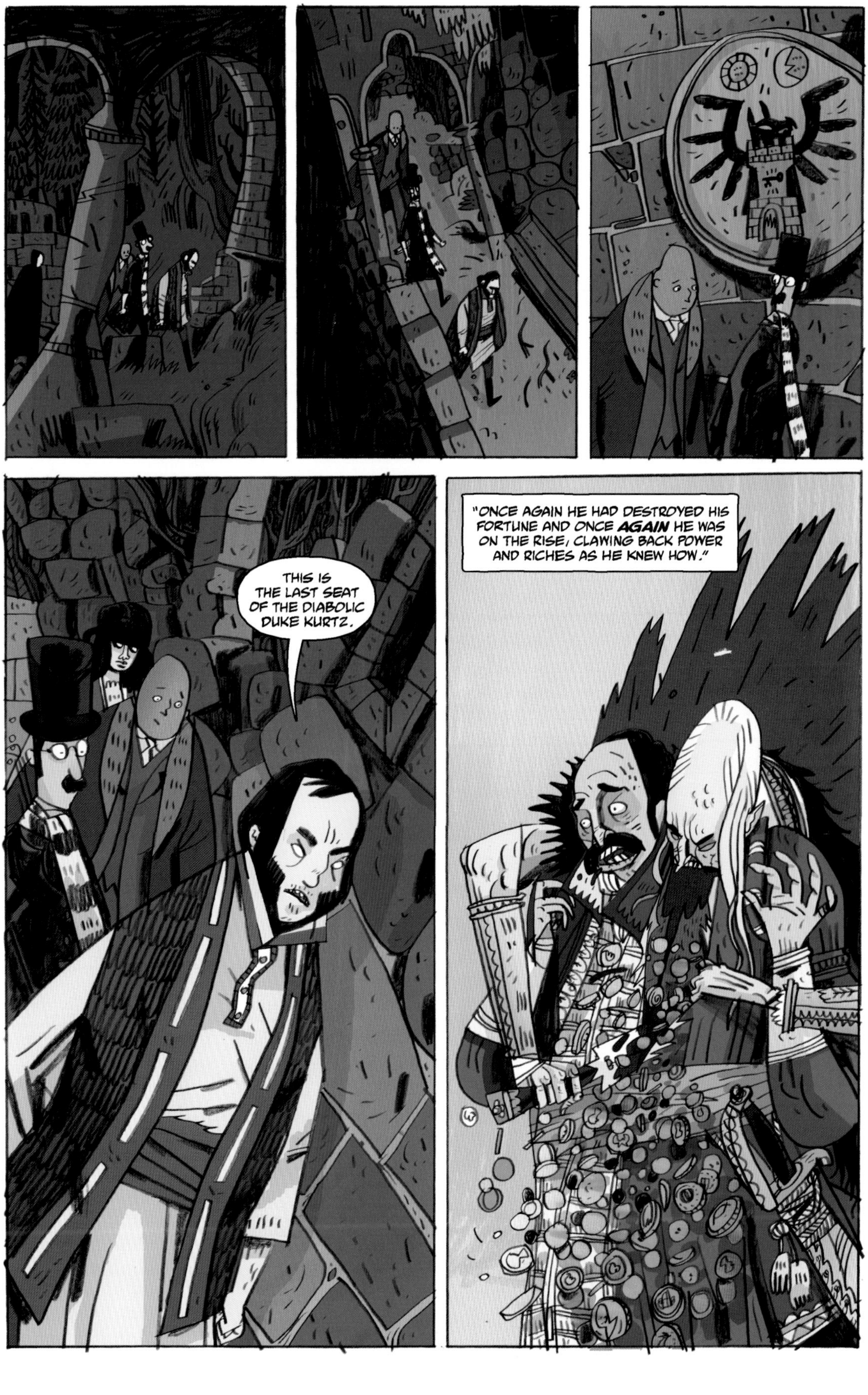
THIS IS THE LAST SEAT OF THE DIABOLIC DUKE KURTZ.
"ONCE AGAIN HE HAD DESTROYED HIS FORTUNE AND ONCE AGAIN HE WAS ON THE RISE, CLAWING BACK POWER AND RICHES AS HE KNEW HOW."

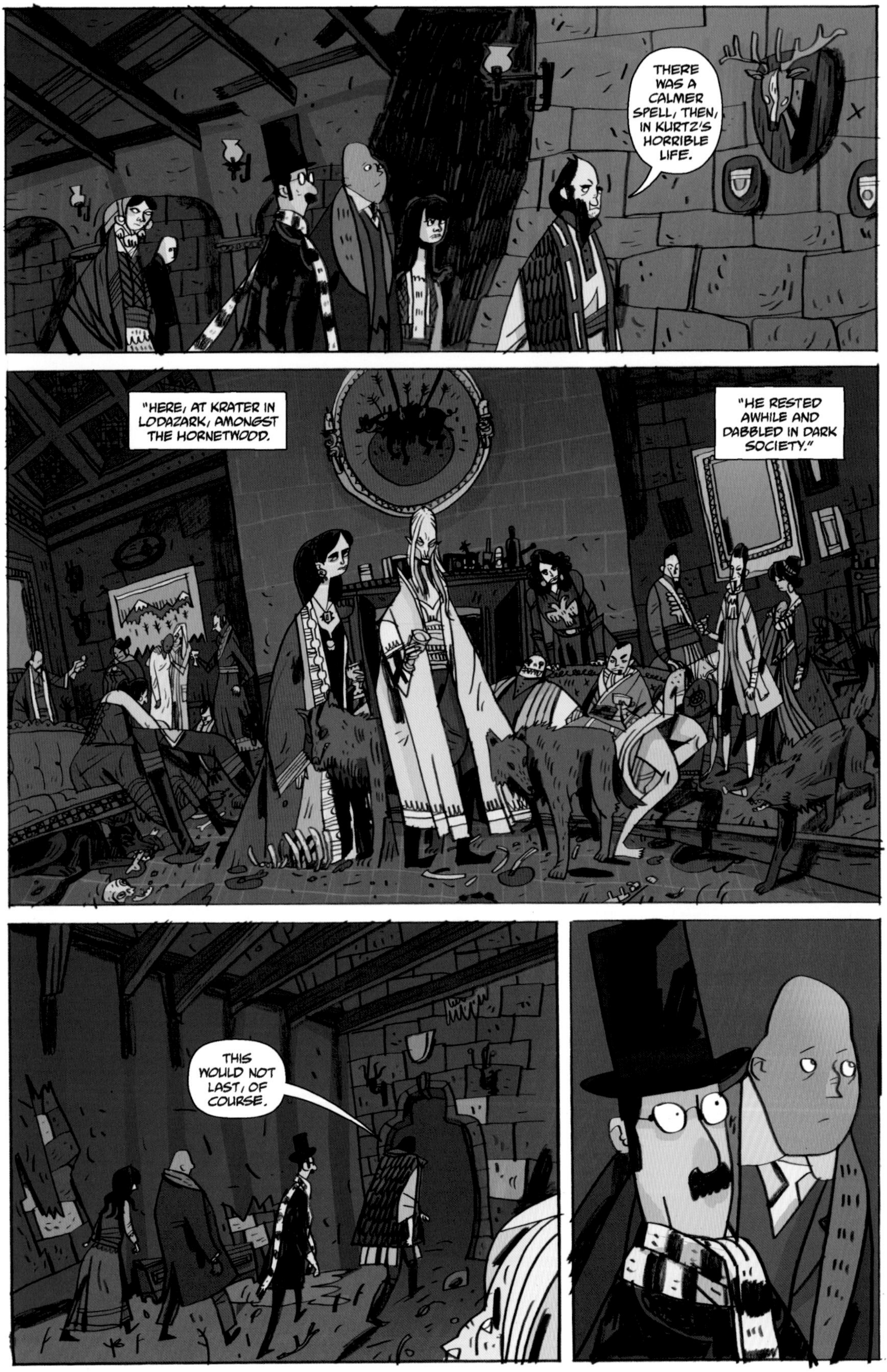
THERE WAS A CALMER SPELL, THEN, IN KURTZ'S HORRIBLE LIFE.
"HERE, AT KRATER IN LODAZARK, AMONGST THE HORNETWOOD.
"HE RESTED AWHILE AND DABBLED IN DARK SOCIETY."
THIS WOULD NOT LAST, OF COURSE.

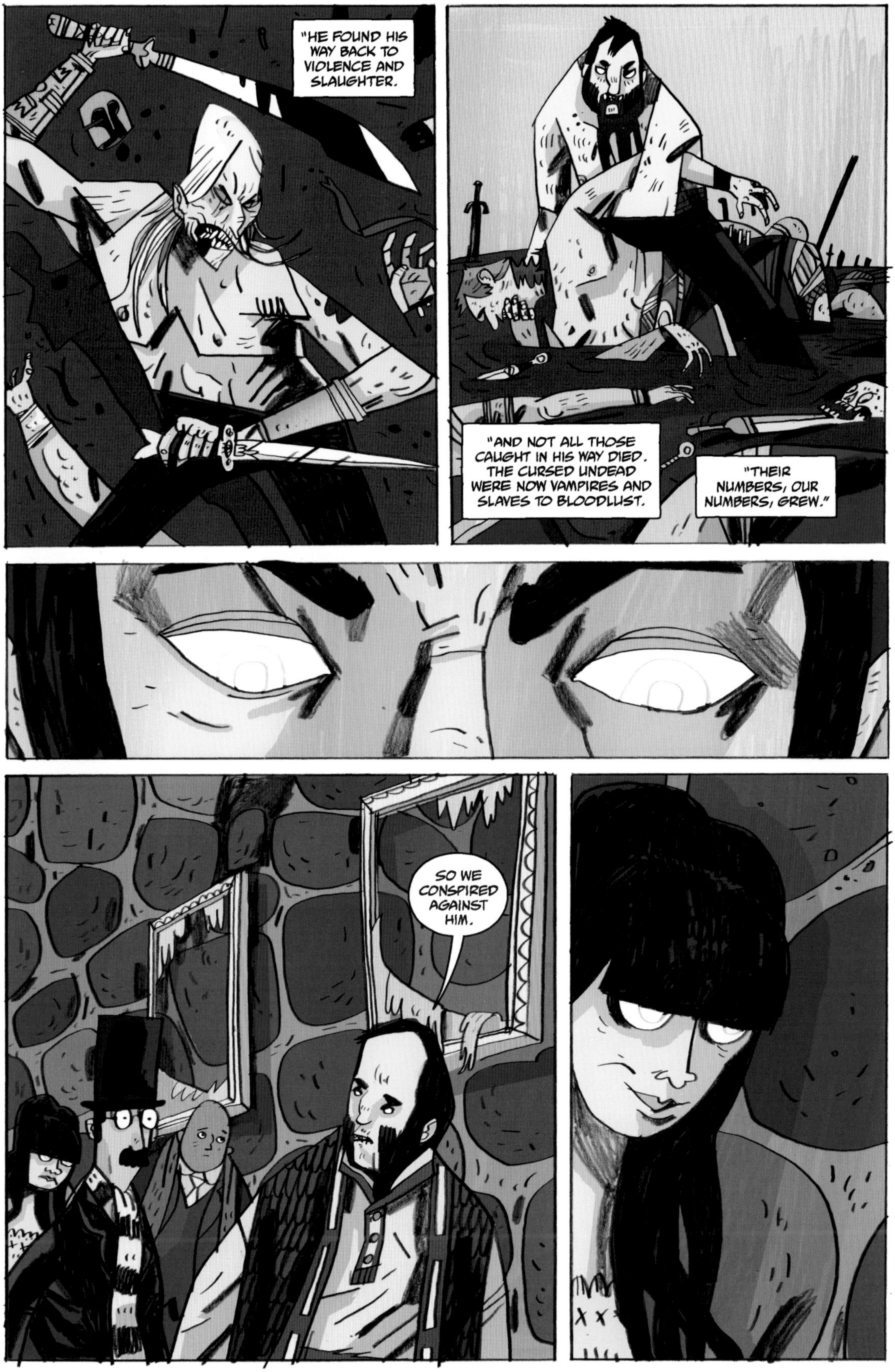
"HE FOUND HIS WAY BACK TO VIOLENCE AND SLAUGHTER.
"AND NOT ALL THOSE CAUGHT IN HIS WAY DIED. THE CURSED UNDEAD WERE NOW VAMPIRES AND SLAVES TO BLOODLUST.
"THEIR NUMBERS, OUR NUMBERS, GREW."
SO WE CONSPIRED AGAINST HIM.

"WE STRUCK A BARGAIN WITH AN OLD BALKAN CLAN TO AID US IN OUR REVENGE."

"THEY WERE HARDY FIGHTERS, ALSO SKILLED CRAFTSMEN."

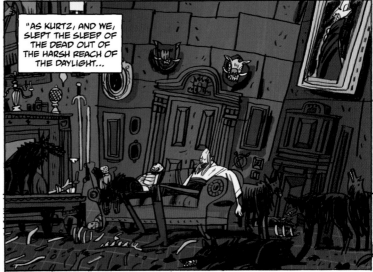

"AS KURTZ, AND WE, SLEPT THE SLEEP OF THE DEAD OUT OF THE HARSH REACH OF THE DAYLIGHT..."

"...THEY ROBBED THE CASTLE OF ITS RICHES."

DINK!

THEY COULD KEEP THE HORDE, EXCEPT FOR THE *SILVER*.

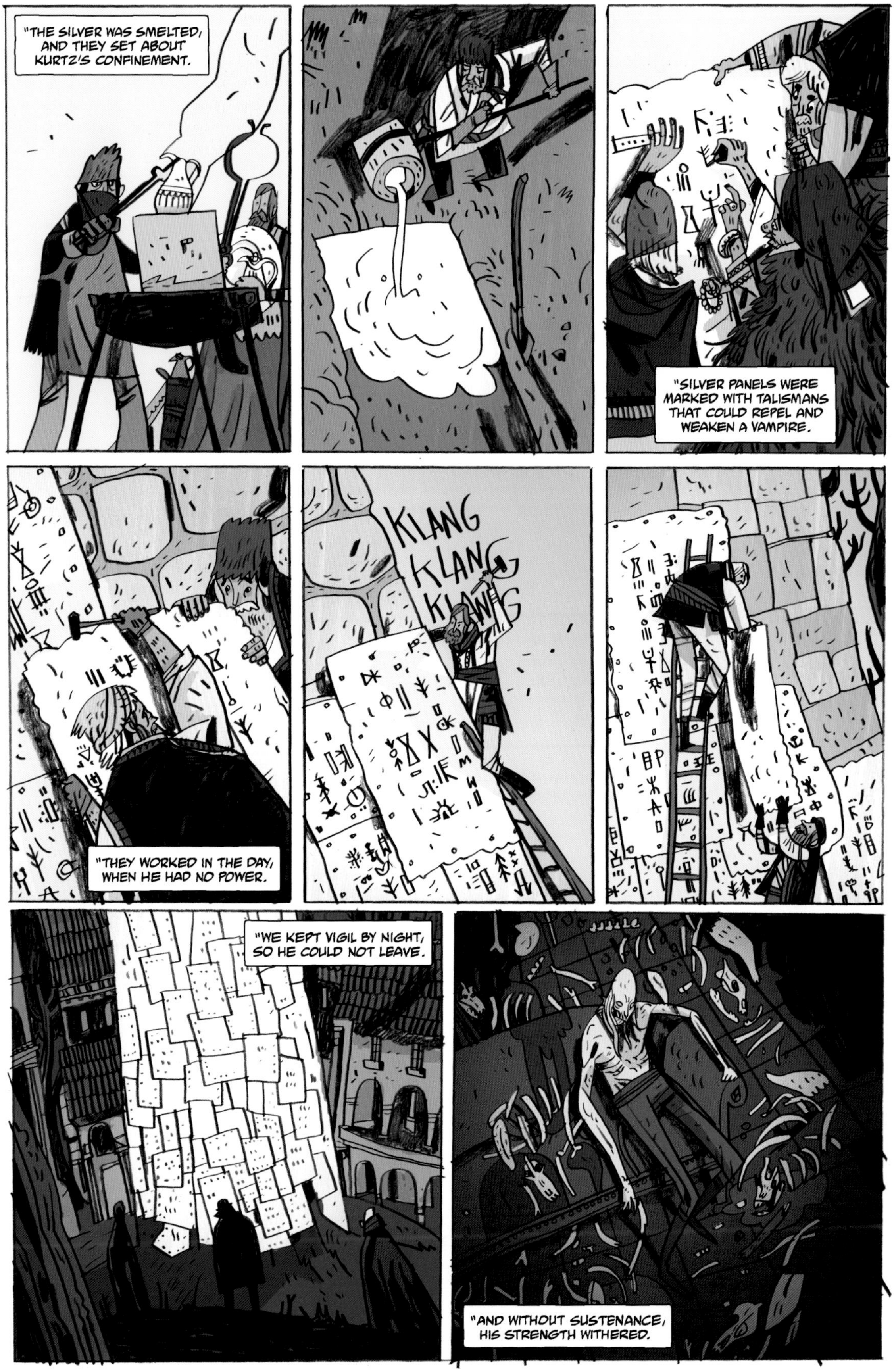
"THE SILVER WAS SMELTED, AND THEY SET ABOUT KURTZ'S CONFINEMENT.
"SILVER PANELS WERE MARKED WITH TALISMANS THAT COULD REPEL AND WEAKEN A VAMPIRE.
"THEY WORKED IN THE DAY, WHEN HE HAD NO POWER.
KLANG KLANG KLANG
"WE KEPT VIGIL BY NIGHT, SO HE COULD NOT LEAVE.
"AND WITHOUT SUSTENANCE, HIS STRENGTH WITHERED.

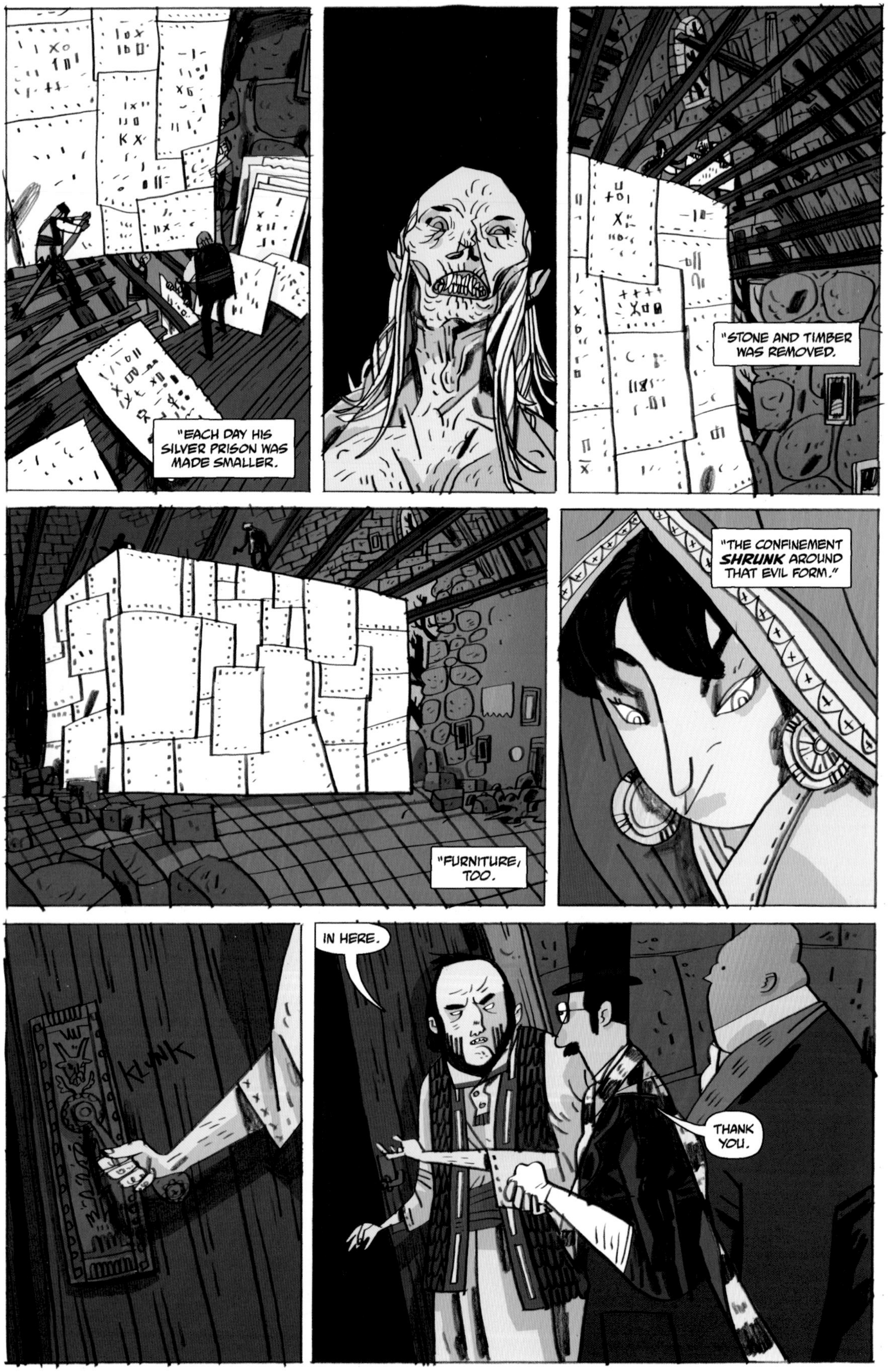
"EACH DAY HIS SILVER PRISON WAS MADE SMALLER.
"STONE AND TIMBER WAS REMOVED.
"FURNITURE, TOO.
"THE CONFINEMENT SHRUNK AROUND THAT EVIL FORM."
KLUNK
IN HERE.
THANK YOU.

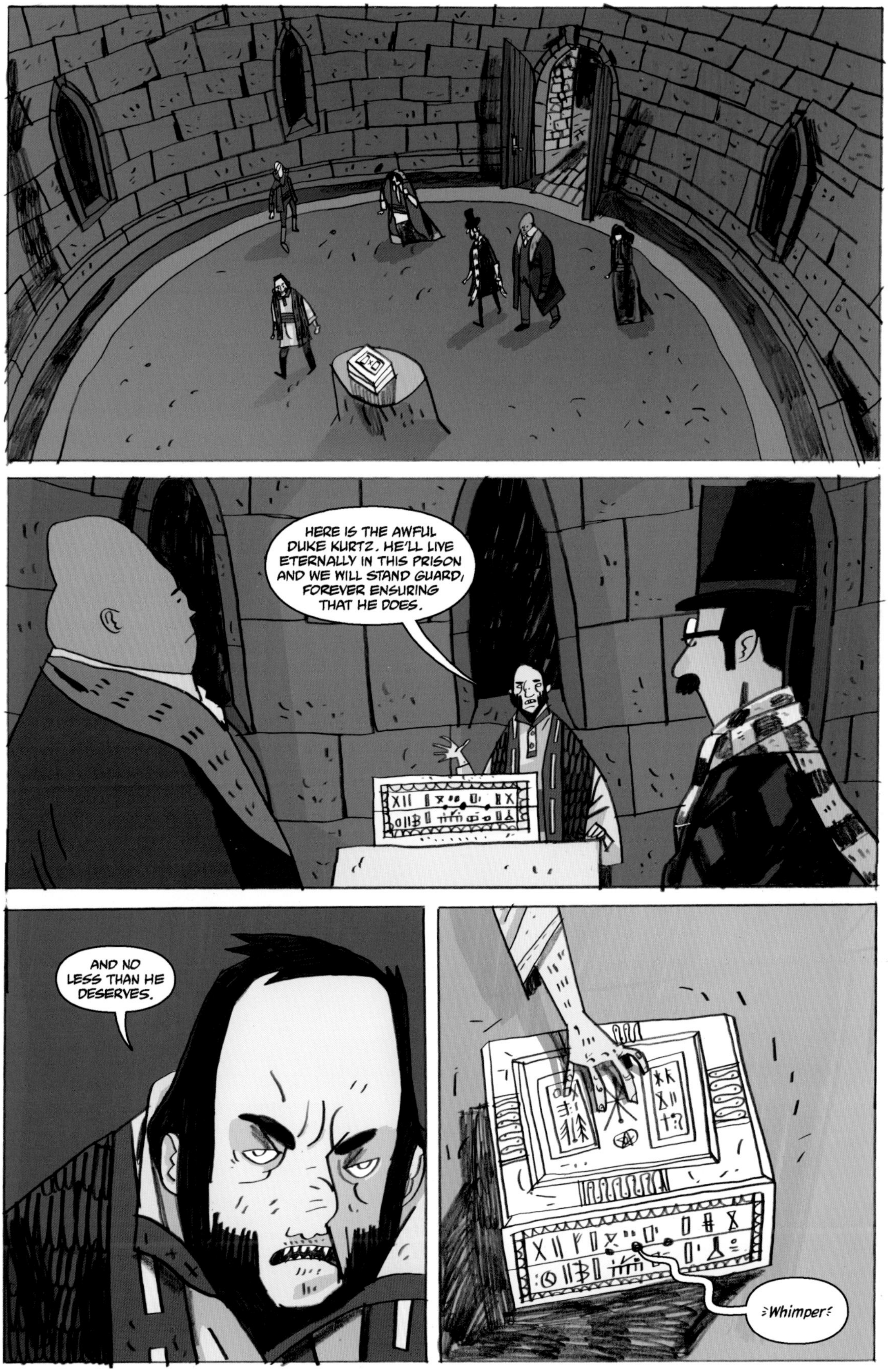
HERE IS THE AWFUL DUKE KURTZ. HE'LL LIVE ETERNALLY IN THIS PRISON AND WE WILL STAND GUARD, FOREVER ENSURING THAT HE DOES.
AND NO LESS THAN HE DESERVES.
Whimper

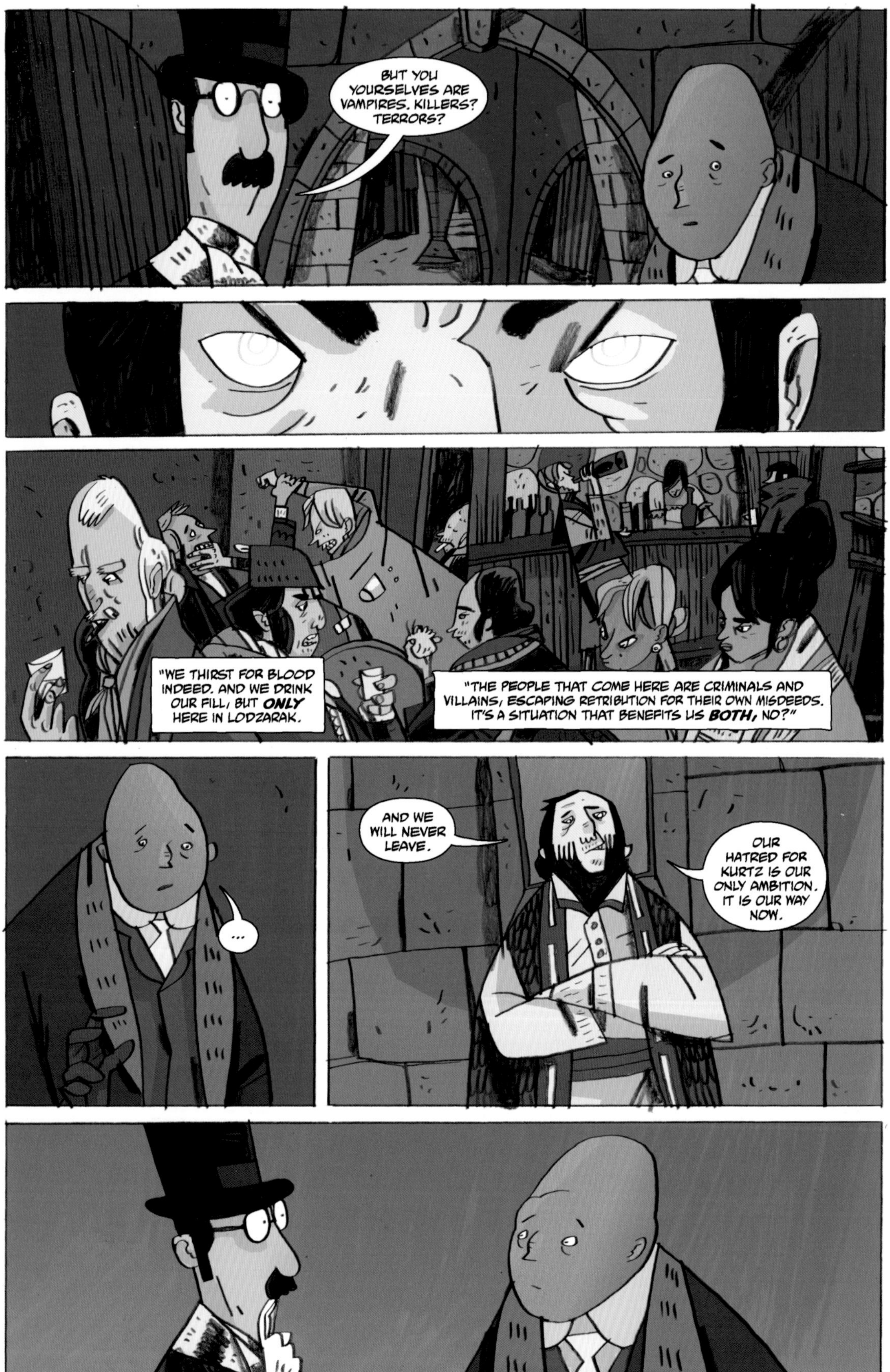
BUT YOU YOURSELVES ARE VAMPIRES. KILLERS? TERRORS?
"WE THIRST FOR BLOOD INDEED. AND WE DRINK OUR FILL, BUT ONLY HERE IN LODZARAK.
"THE PEOPLE THAT COME HERE ARE CRIMINALS AND VILLAINS, ESCAPING RETRIBUTION FOR THEIR OWN MISDEEDS. IT'S A SITUATION THAT BENEFITS US BOTH, NO?"
...
AND WE WILL NEVER LEAVE.
OUR HATRED FOR KURTZ IS OUR ONLY AMBITION. IT IS OUR WAY NOW.

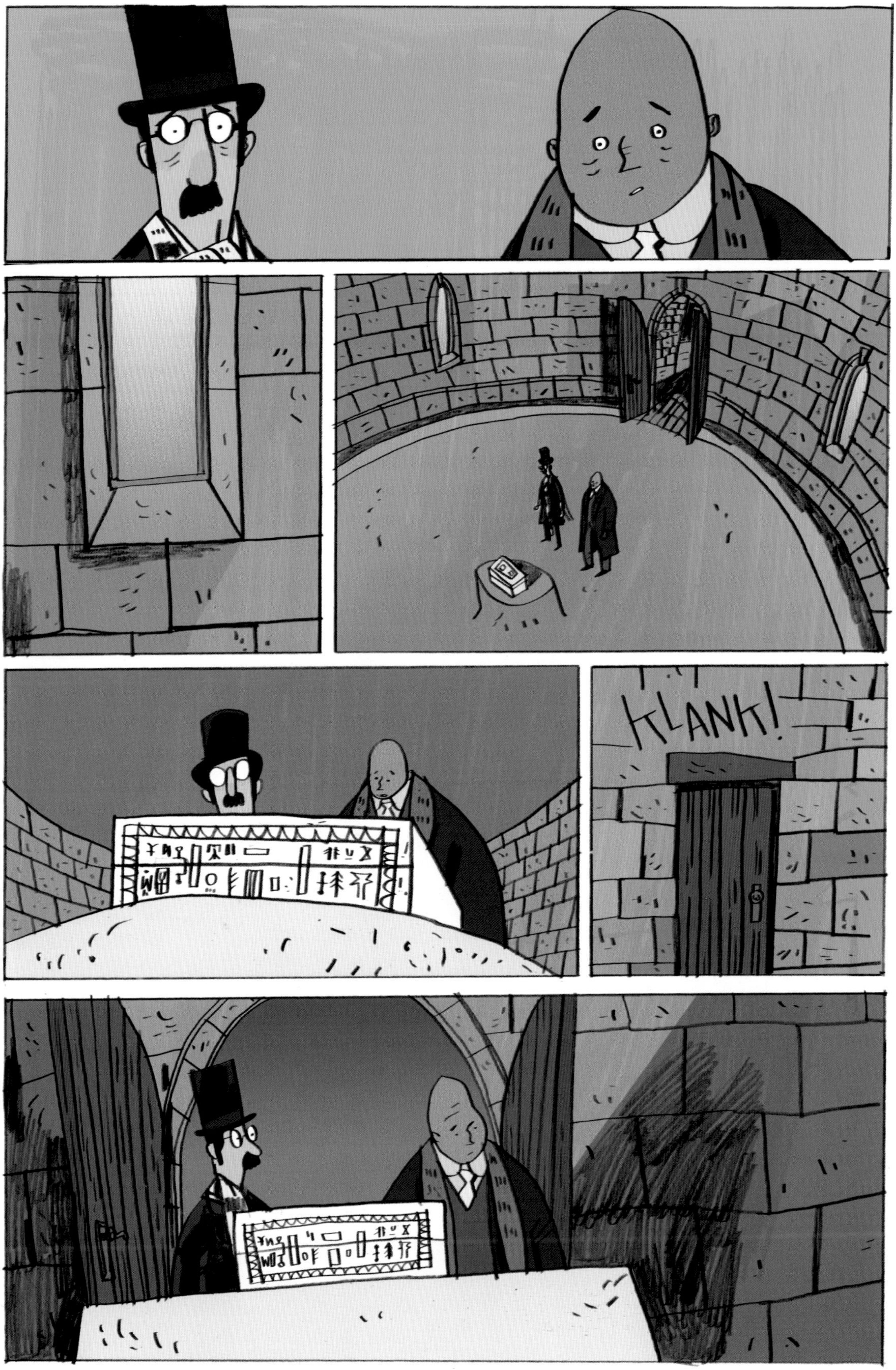

KLANK!

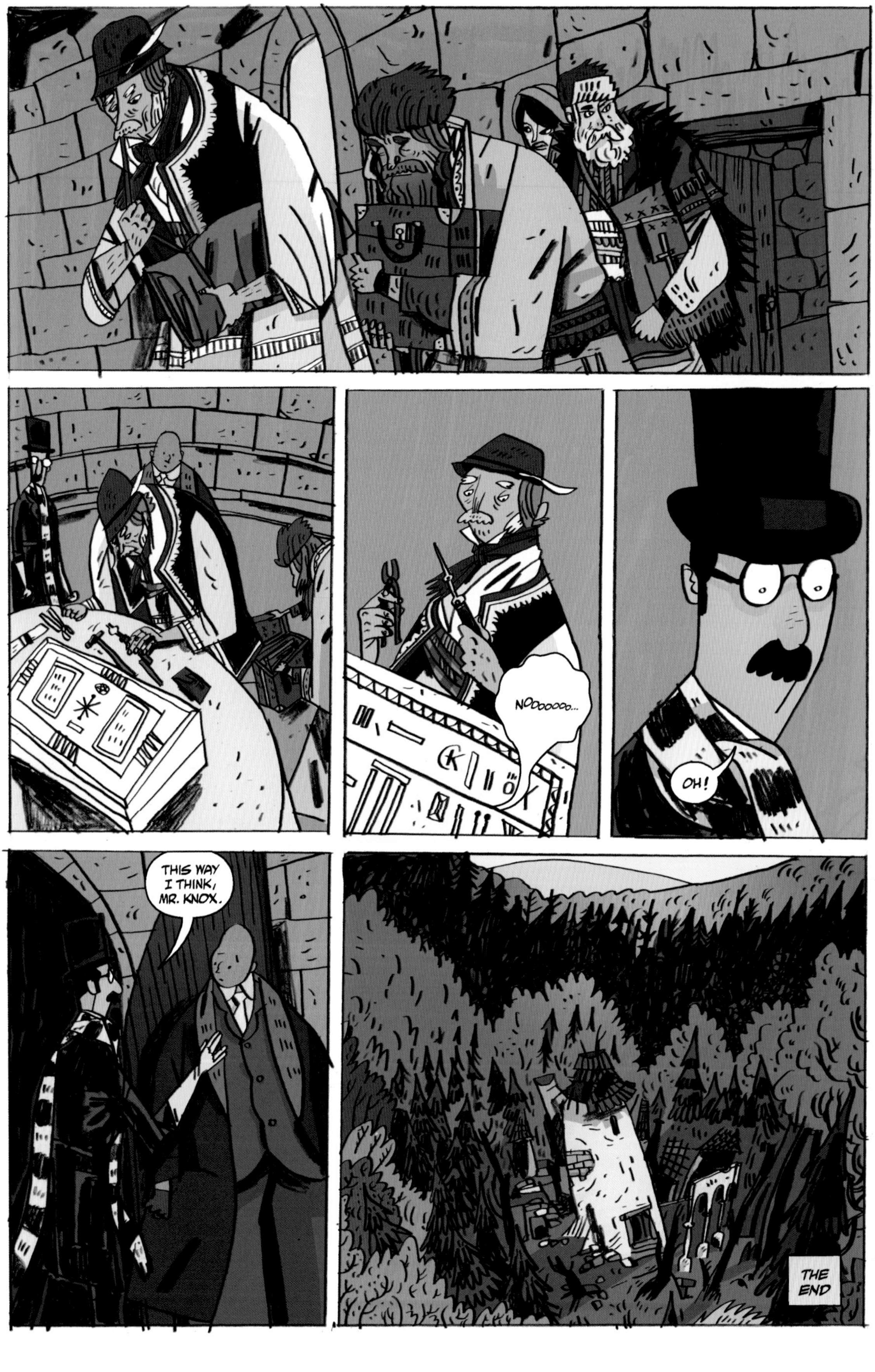
NOOOOOOO...
OH!
THIS WAY I THINK, MR. KNOX.
THE END

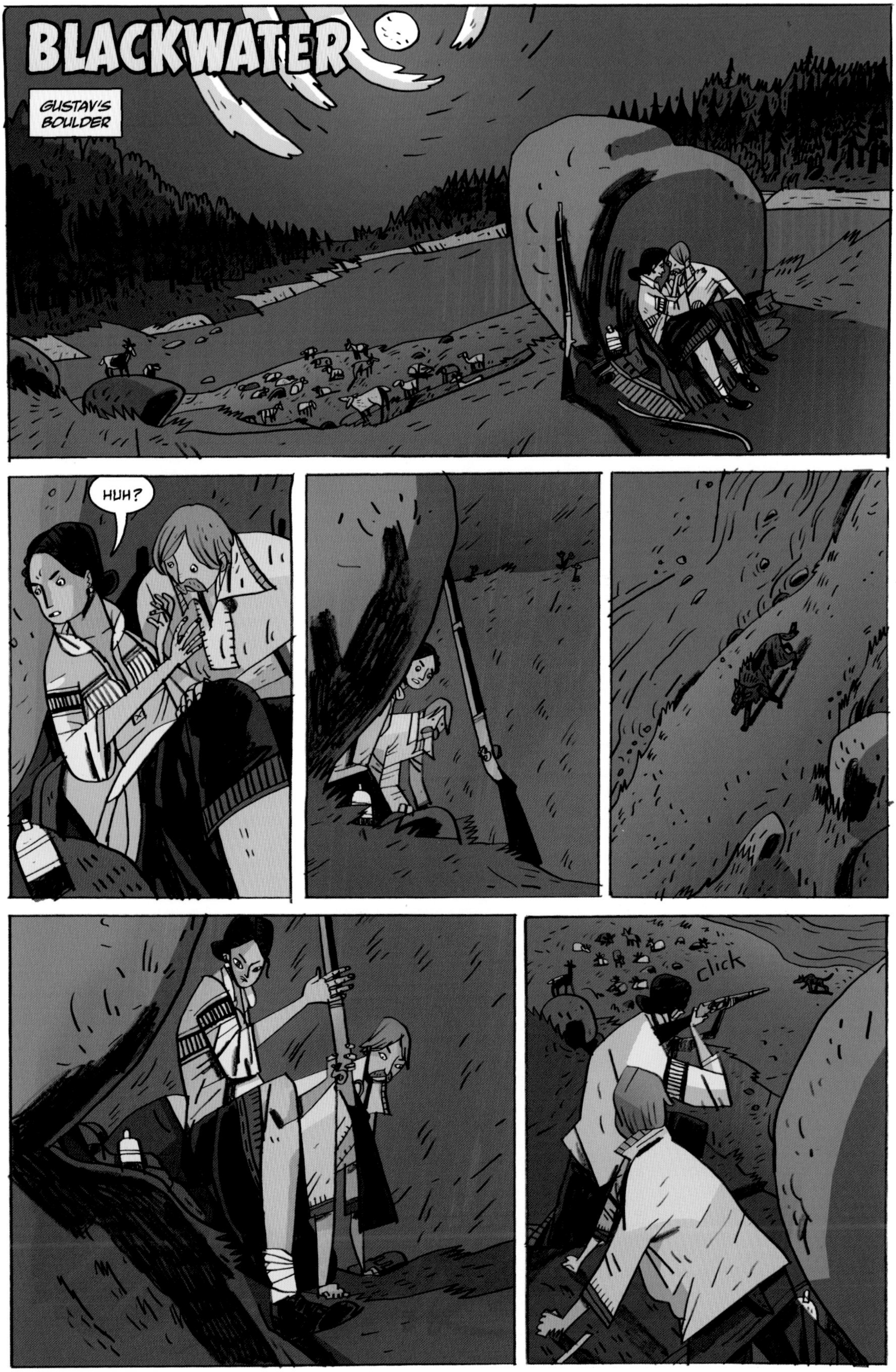
BLACKWATER
GUSTAV'S BOULDER
HUH?
click

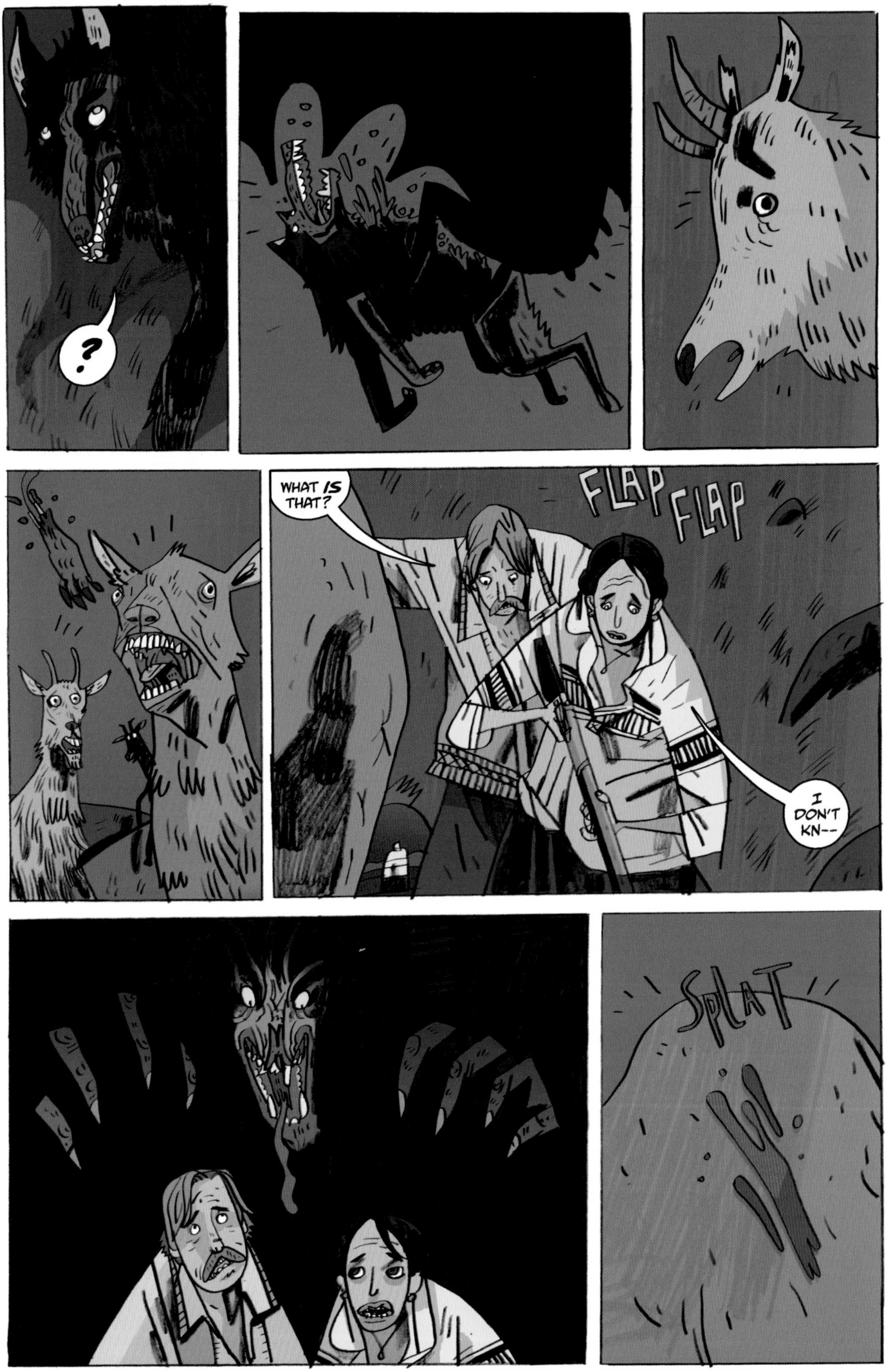
?
WHAT IS THAT?
FLAP FLAP
I DON'T KN--
SPLAT

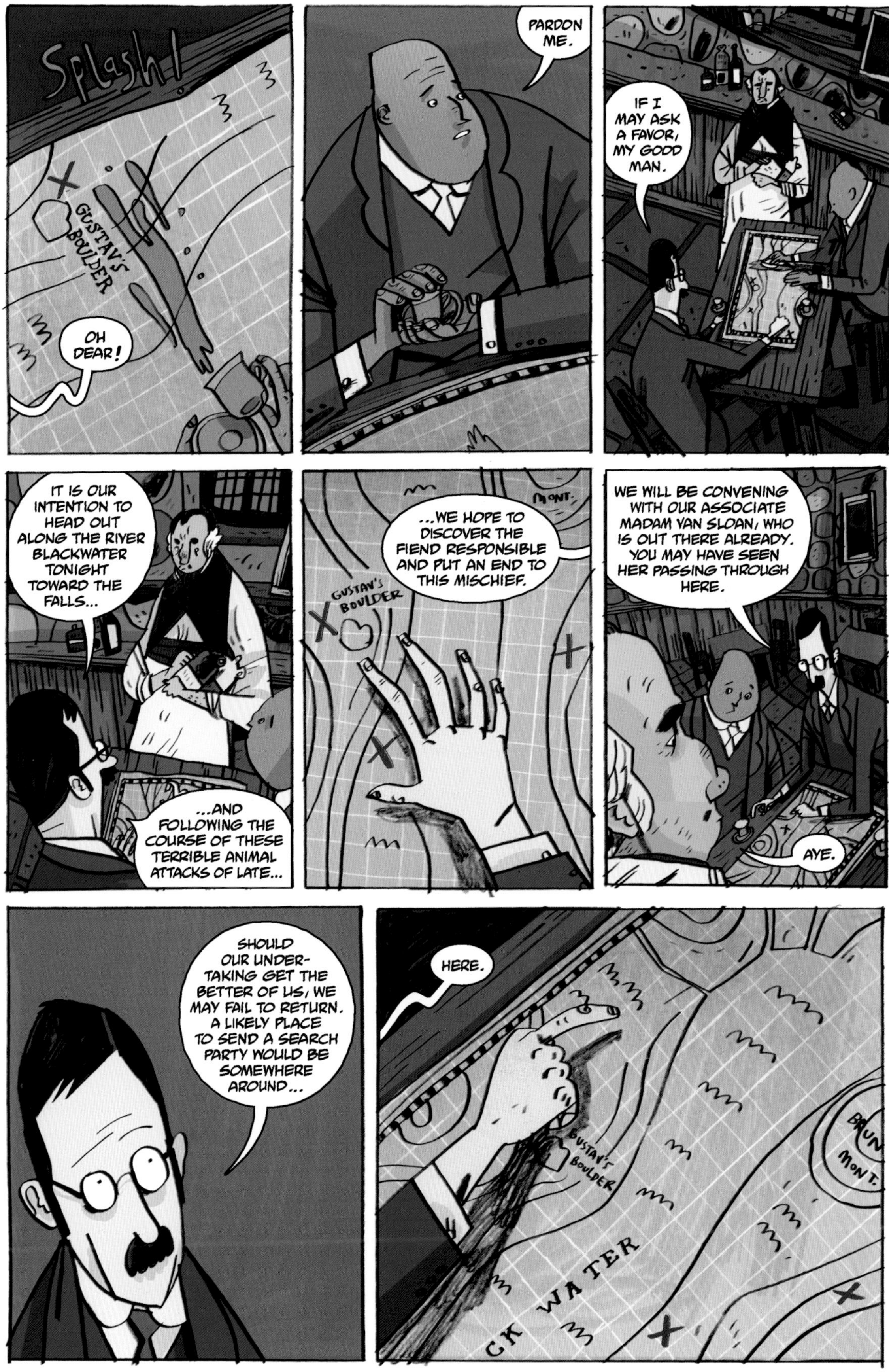
Splash!
GUSTAV'S BOULDER
OH DEAR!
PARDON ME.
IF I MAY ASK A FAVOR, MY GOOD MAN.
IT IS OUR INTENTION TO HEAD OUT ALONG THE RIVER BLACKWATER TONIGHT TOWARD THE FALLS...
...AND FOLLOWING THE COURSE OF THESE TERRIBLE ANIMAL ATTACKS OF LATE...
MONT.
...WE HOPE TO DISCOVER THE FIEND RESPONSIBLE AND PUT AN END TO THIS MISCHIEF.
GUSTAV'S BOULDER
WE WILL BE CONVENING WITH OUR ASSOCIATE MADAM VAN SLOAN, WHO IS OUT THERE ALREADY. YOU MAY HAVE SEEN HER PASSING THROUGH HERE.
AYE.
SHOULD OUR UNDER-TAKING GET THE BETTER OF US, WE MAY FAIL TO RETURN. A LIKELY PLACE TO SEND A SEARCH PARTY WOULD BE SOMEWHERE AROUND...
HERE.
GUSTAV'S BOULDER
BRUN MONT.
CK WATER

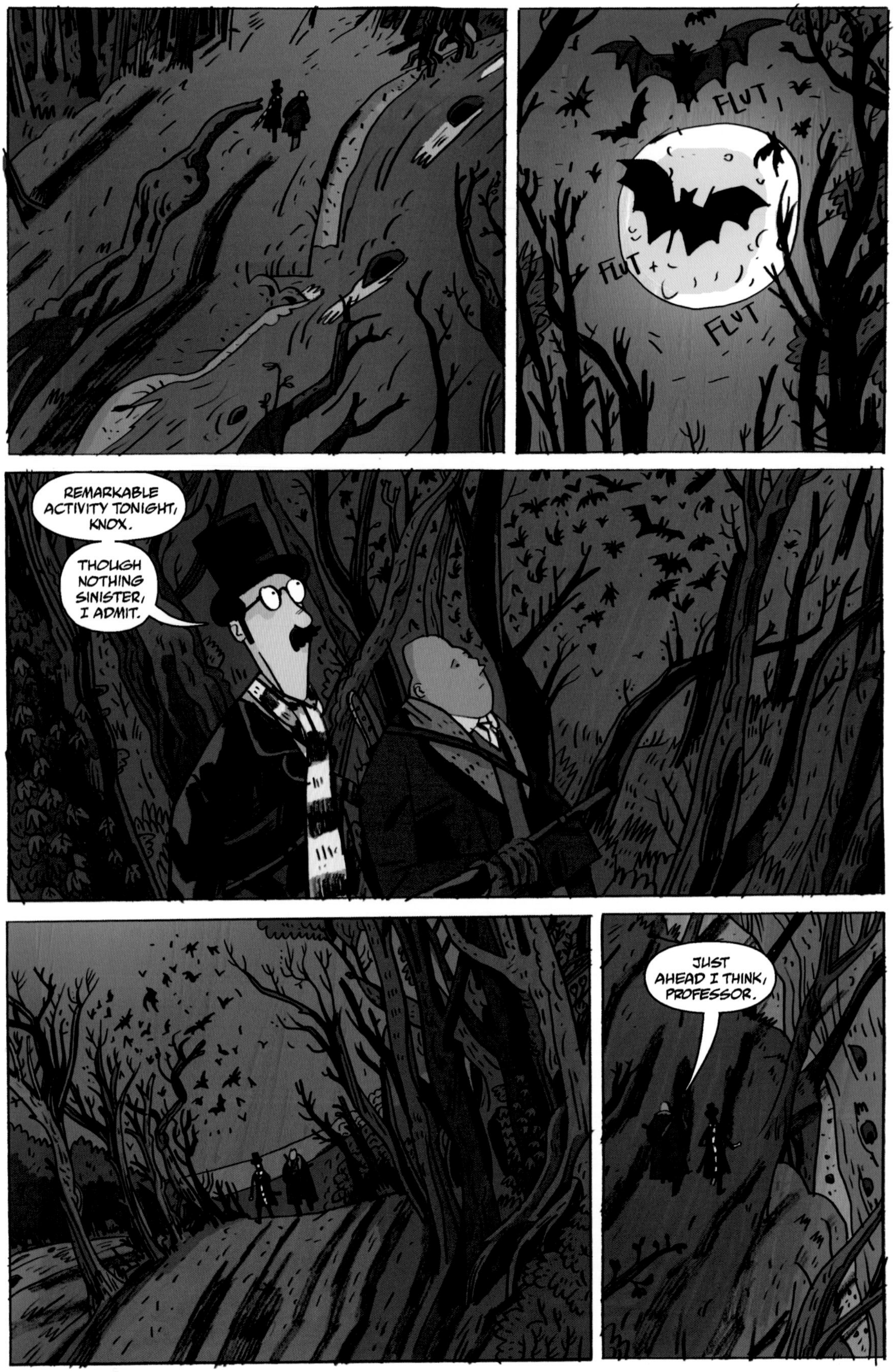
FLUT
FLUT
FLUT
REMARKABLE ACTIVITY TONIGHT, KNOX.
THOUGH NOTHING SINISTER, I ADMIT.
JUST AHEAD I THINK, PROFESSOR.

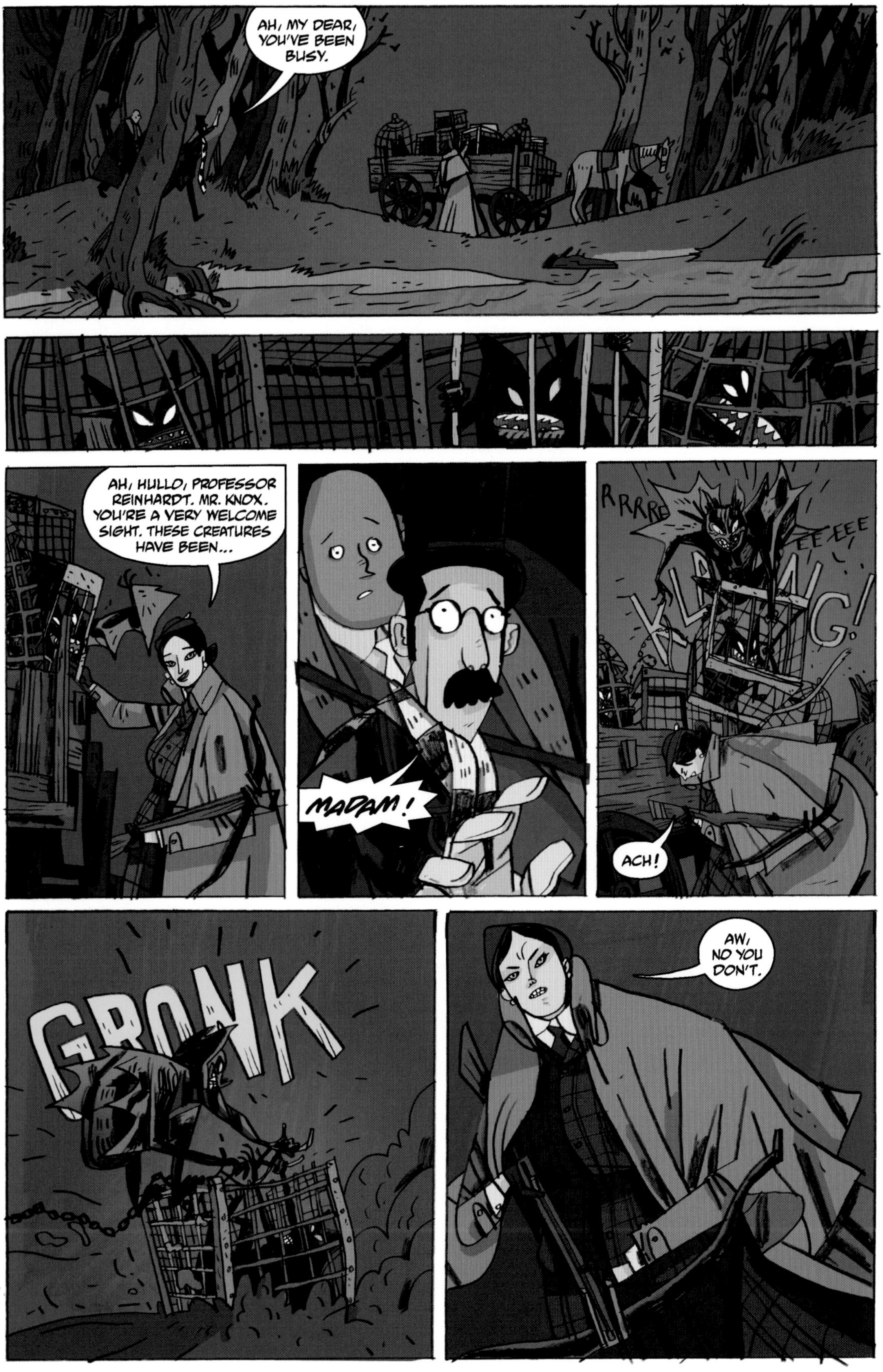
AH, MY DEAR, YOU'VE BEEN BUSY.
AH, HULLO, PROFESSOR REINHARDT. MR. KNOX. YOU'RE A VERY WELCOME SIGHT. THESE CREATURES HAVE BEEN...
MADAM!
RRRRE
EE EEE
ACH!
GRONK
AW, NO YOU DON'T.

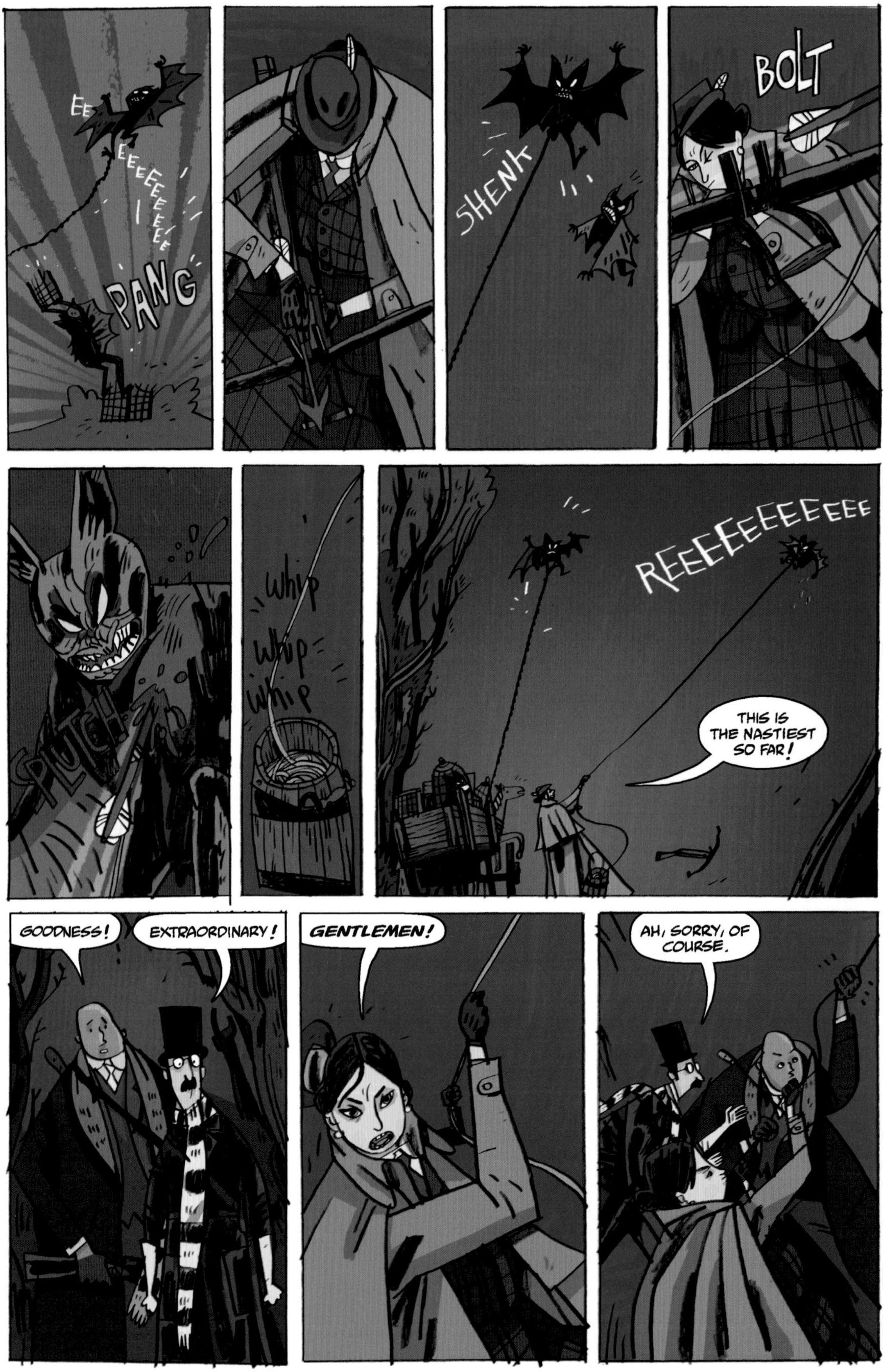
EE
EEEEEEEEE
PANG
SHENK
BOLT
SPLUTCH
WHIP
WHIP
WHIP
REEEEEEEEEEE
THIS IS THE NASTIEST SO FAR!
GOODNESS!
EXTRAORDINARY!
GENTLEMEN!
AH, SORRY, OF COURSE.

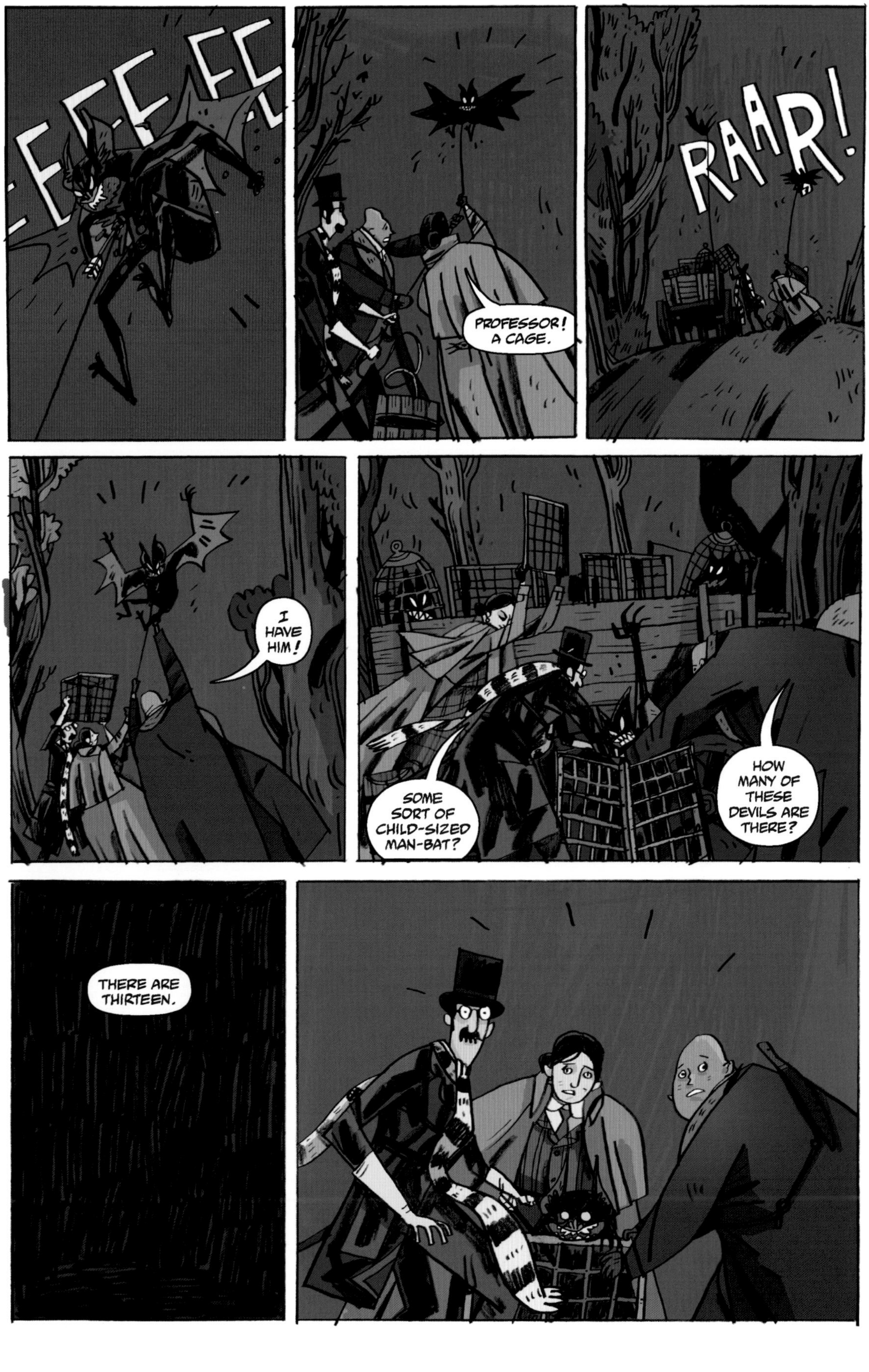
EEEEEEE
PROFESSOR! A CAGE.
RAAR!
I HAVE HIM!
SOME SORT OF CHILD-SIZED MAN-BAT?
HOW MANY OF THESE DEVILS ARE THERE?
THERE ARE THIRTEEN.

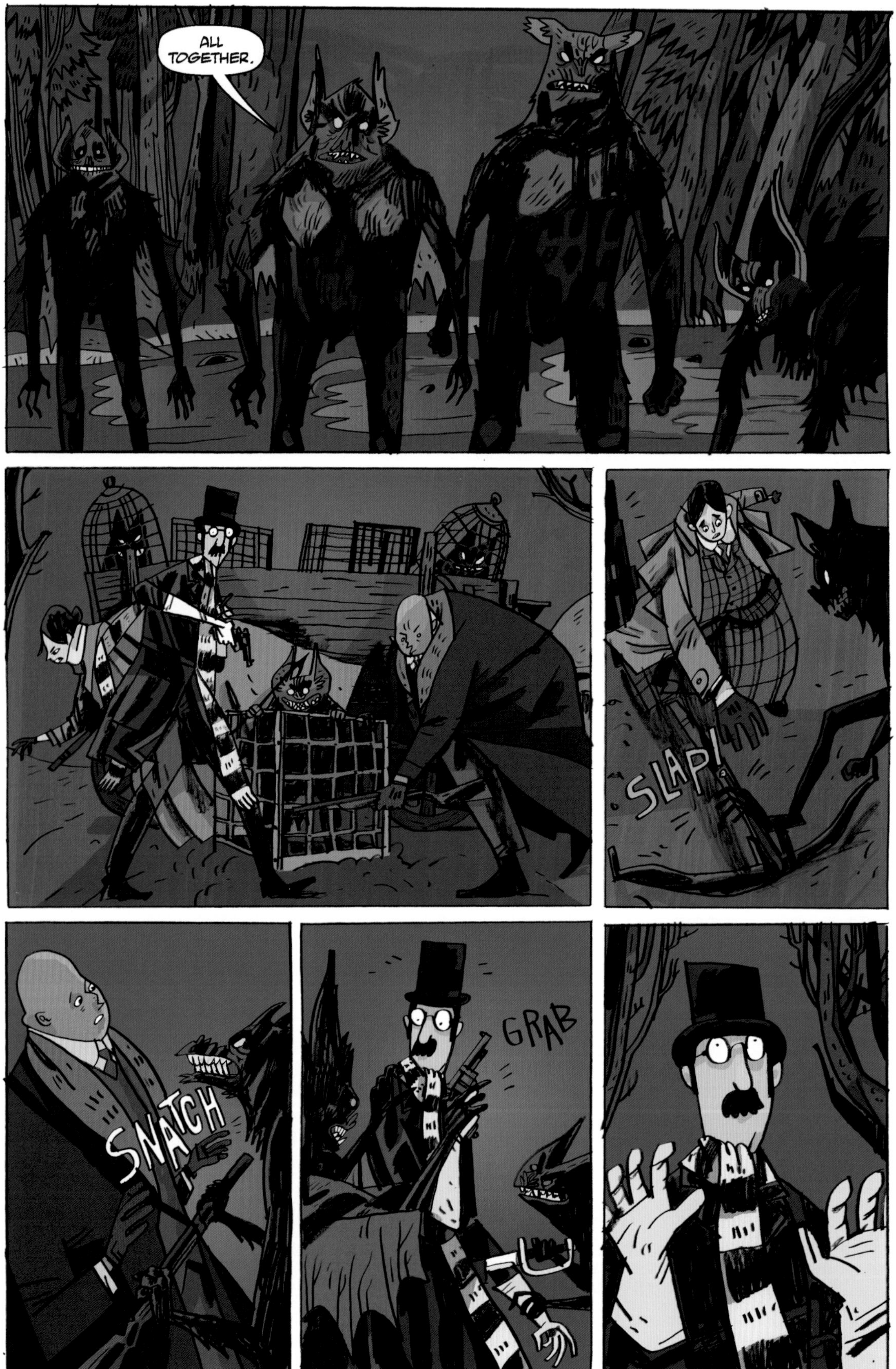
ALL TOGETHER.
SLAP!
SNATCH
GRAB

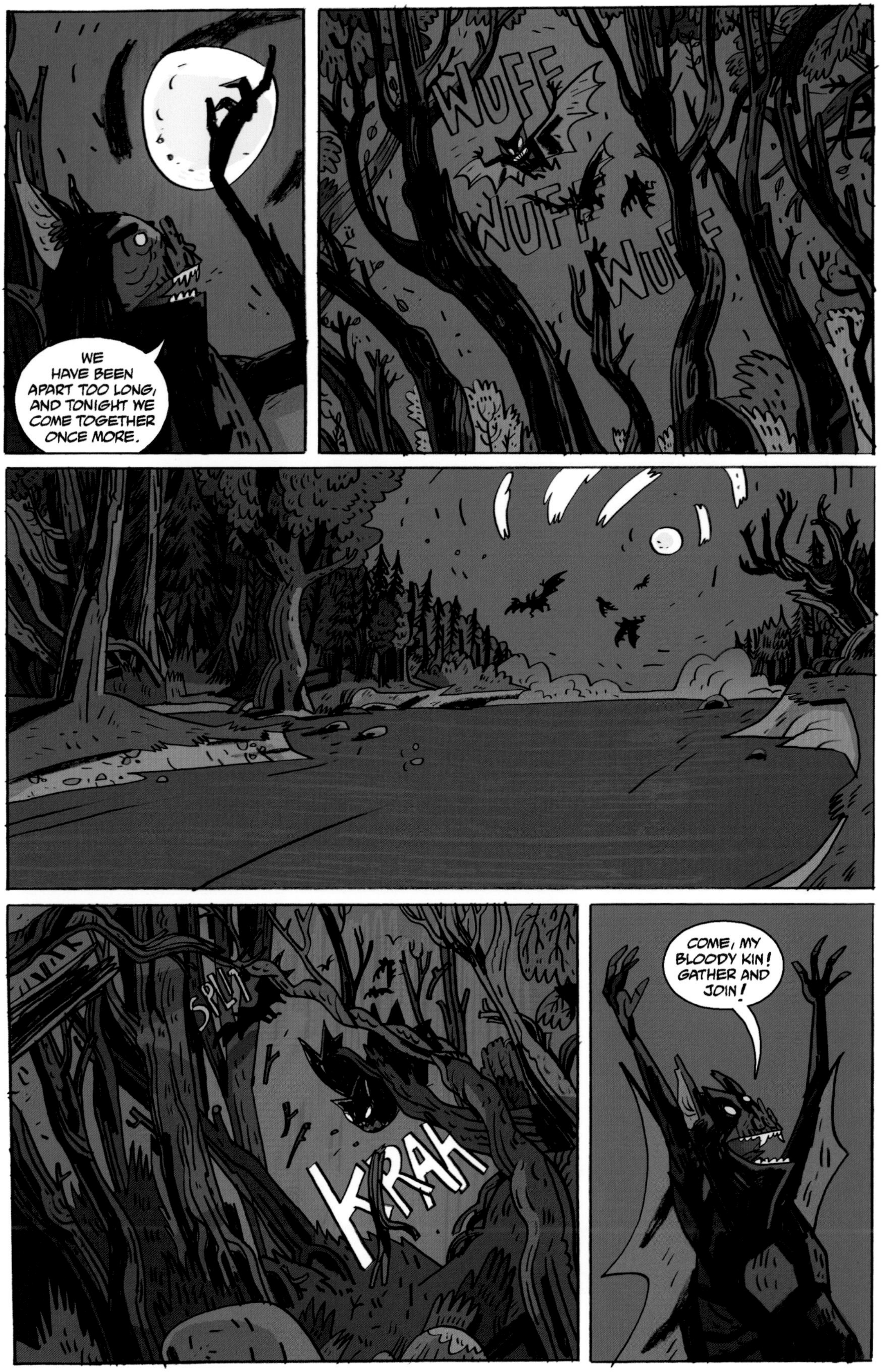
WE HAVE BEEN APART TOO LONG, AND TONIGHT WE COME TOGETHER ONCE MORE.
WUFF
WUFF
WUFF
SPLT
KRAH
COME, MY BLOODY KIN! GATHER AND JOIN!

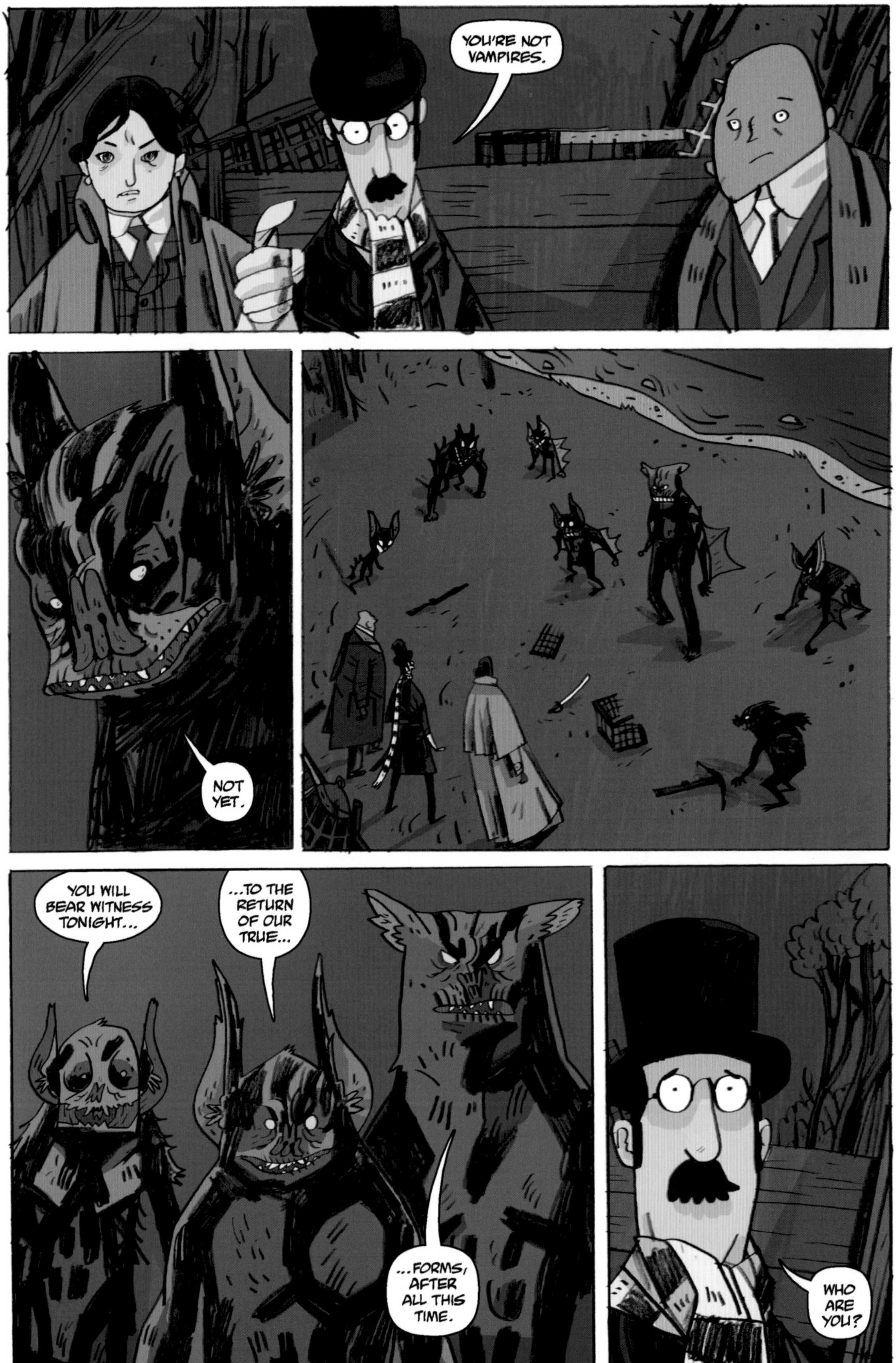
YOU'RE NOT VAMPIRES.
NOT YET.
YOU WILL BEAR WITNESS TONIGHT...
...TO THE RETURN OF OUR TRUE...
...FORMS, AFTER ALL THIS TIME.
WHO ARE YOU?

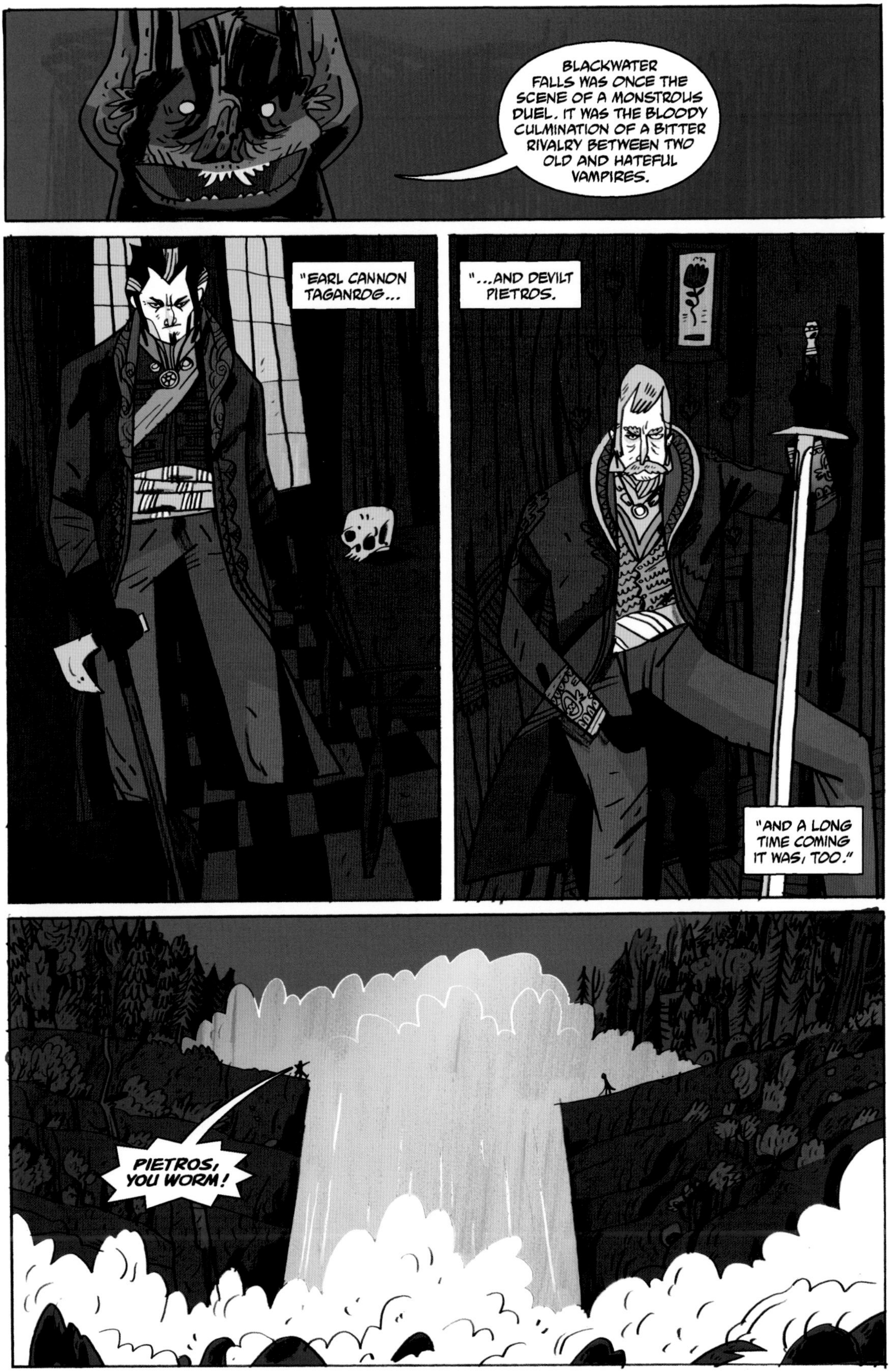
BLACKWATER FALLS WAS ONCE THE SCENE OF A MONSTROUS DUEL. IT WAS THE BLOODY CULMINATION OF A BITTER RIVALRY BETWEEN TWO OLD AND HATEFUL VAMPIRES.
"EARL CANNON TAGANROG...
"...AND DEVILT PIETROS.
"AND A LONG TIME COMING IT WAS, TOO."
PIETROS, YOU WORM!

"TONIGHT I WILL PUT AN END TO YOU!"

"TAGANROG, YOU SLIPPERY EEL!"

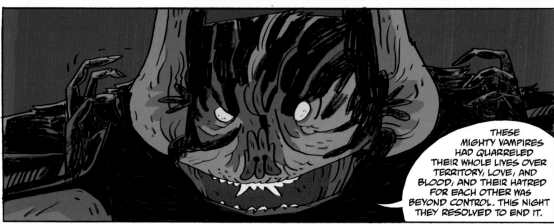

THESE MIGHTY VAMPIRES HAD QUARRELED THEIR WHOLE LIVES OVER TERRITORY, LOVE, AND BLOOD, AND THEIR HATRED FOR EACH OTHER WAS BEYOND CONTROL. THIS NIGHT THEY RESOLVED TO END IT.

AAAARRGGH!

AAAIIIEEEE!

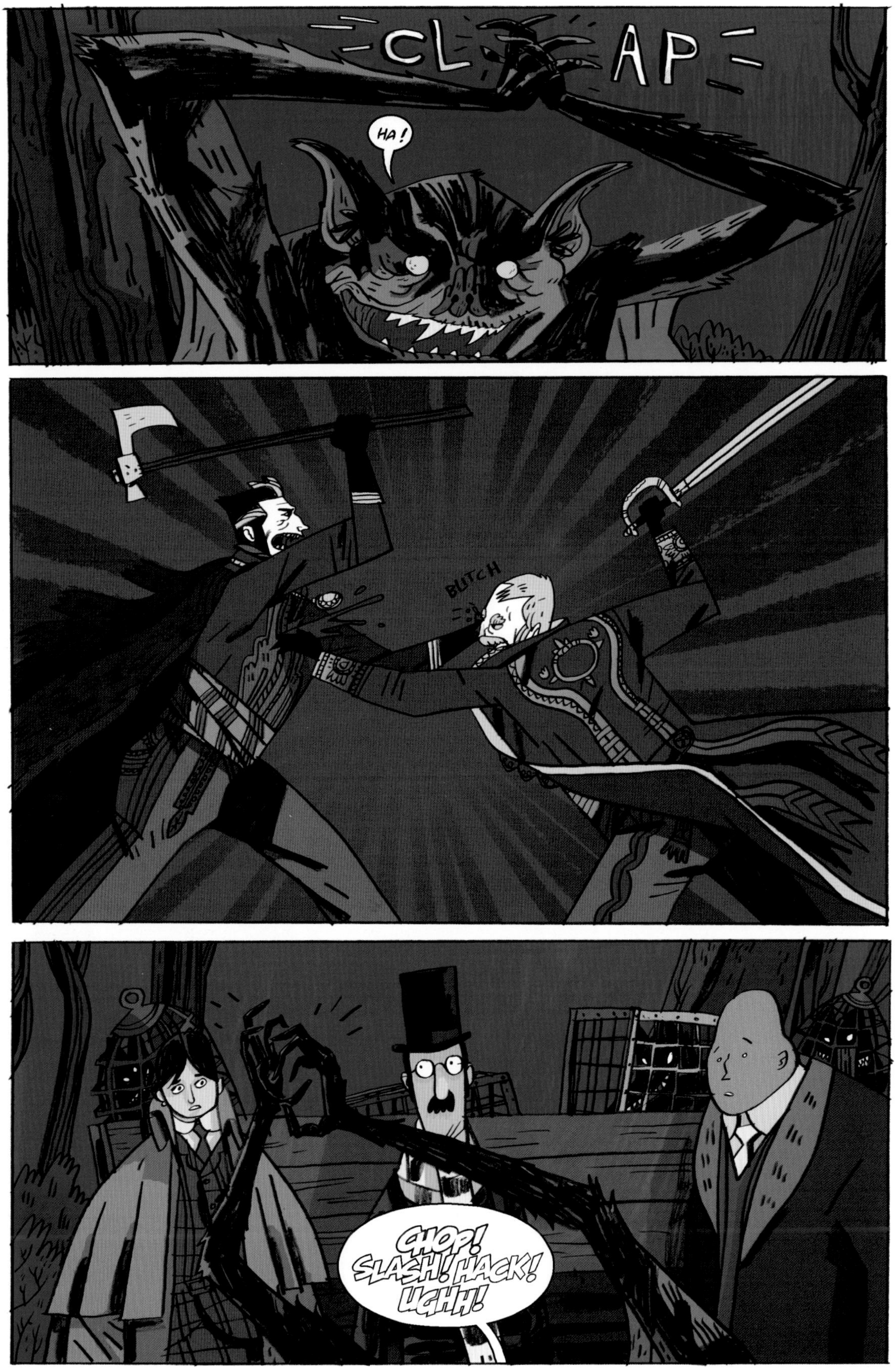
CL AP
HA!
BLITCH
CHOP! SLASH! HACK! UGHH!

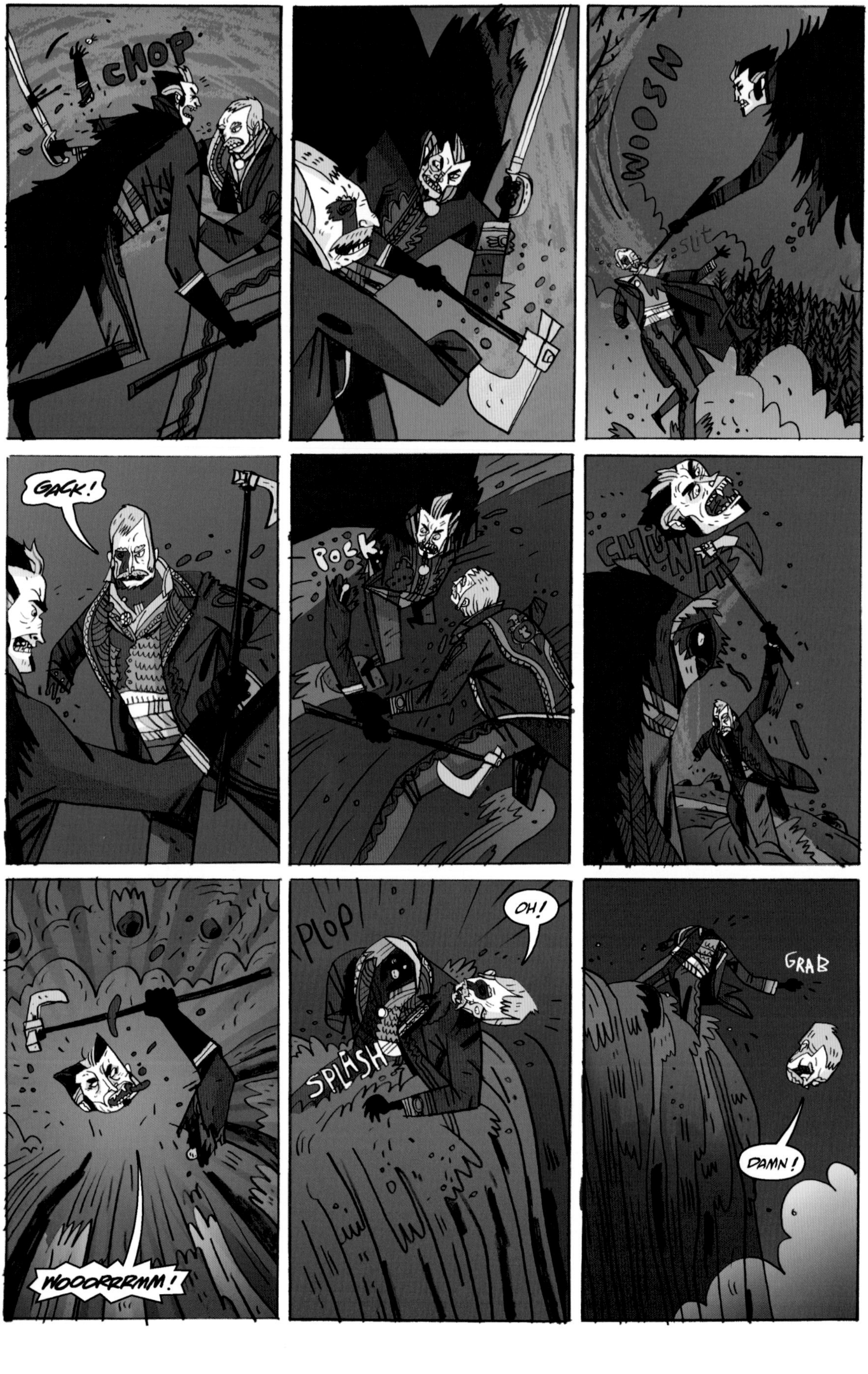
CHOP
WOOSH
SLIT
GACK!
POCK
CHUNK
WOOORRRMM!
PLOP
OH!
SPLASH
GRAB
DAMN!

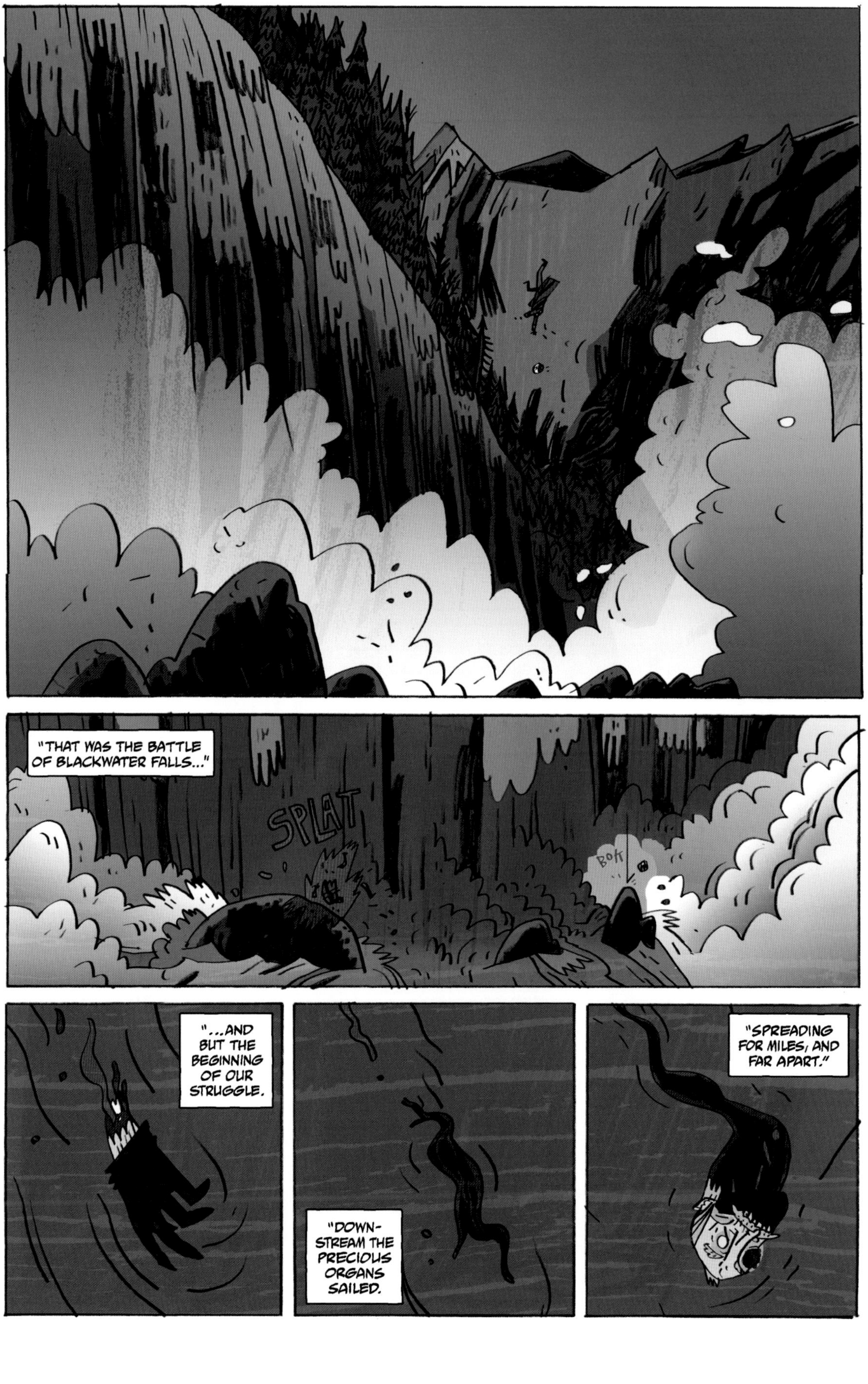
"THAT WAS THE BATTLE OF BLACKWATER FALLS..."
SPLAT
BOK
"...AND BUT THE BEGINNING OF OUR STRUGGLE.
"DOWN-STREAM THE PRECIOUS ORGANS SAILED.
"SPREADING FOR MILES, AND FAR APART."

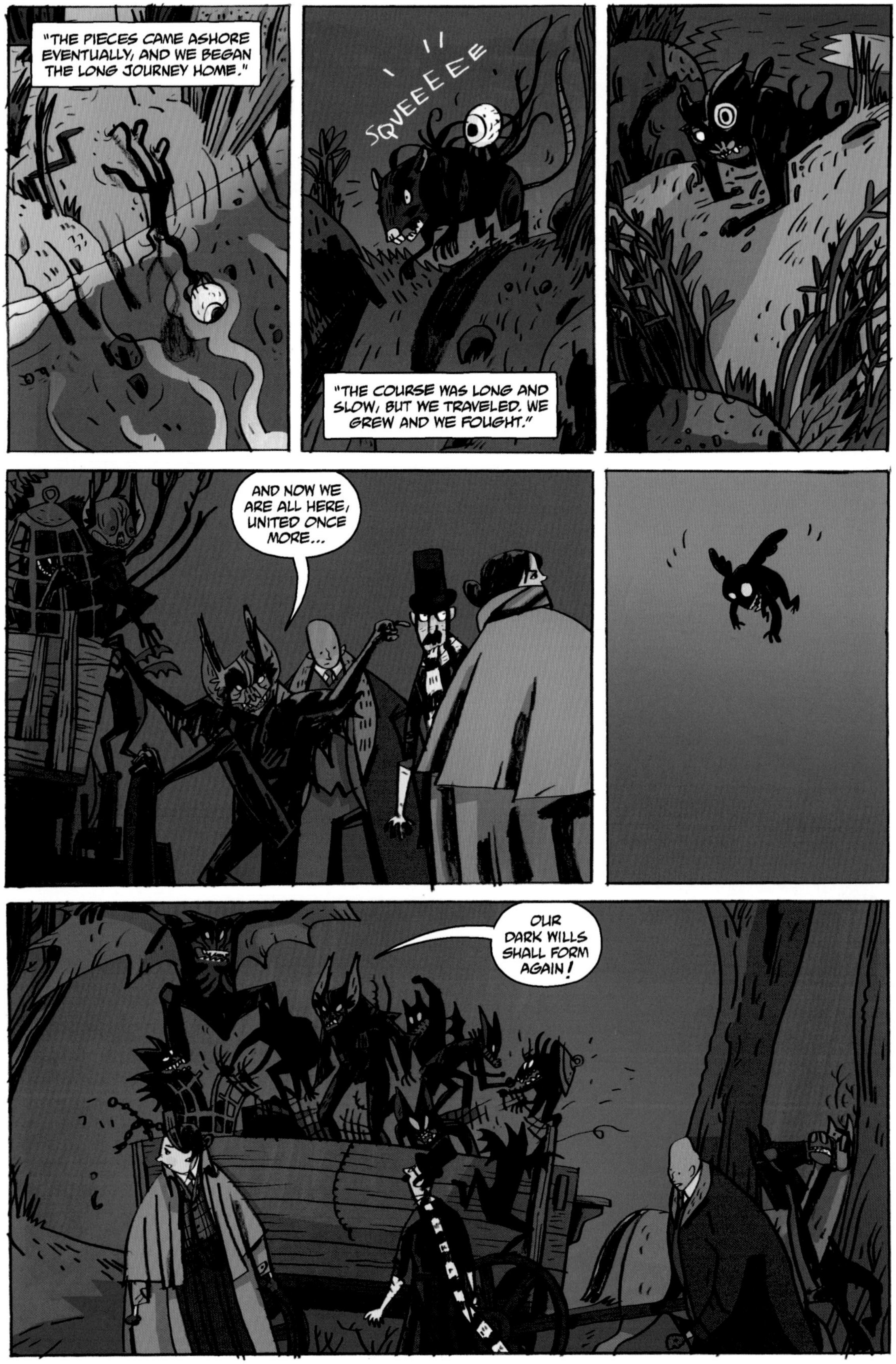
"THE PIECES CAME ASHORE EVENTUALLY, AND WE BEGAN THE LONG JOURNEY HOME."
SQVEEEEE
"THE COURSE WAS LONG AND SLOW, BUT WE TRAVELED. WE GREW AND WE FOUGHT."
AND NOW WE ARE ALL HERE, UNITED ONCE MORE...
OUR DARK WILLS SHALL FORM AGAIN!

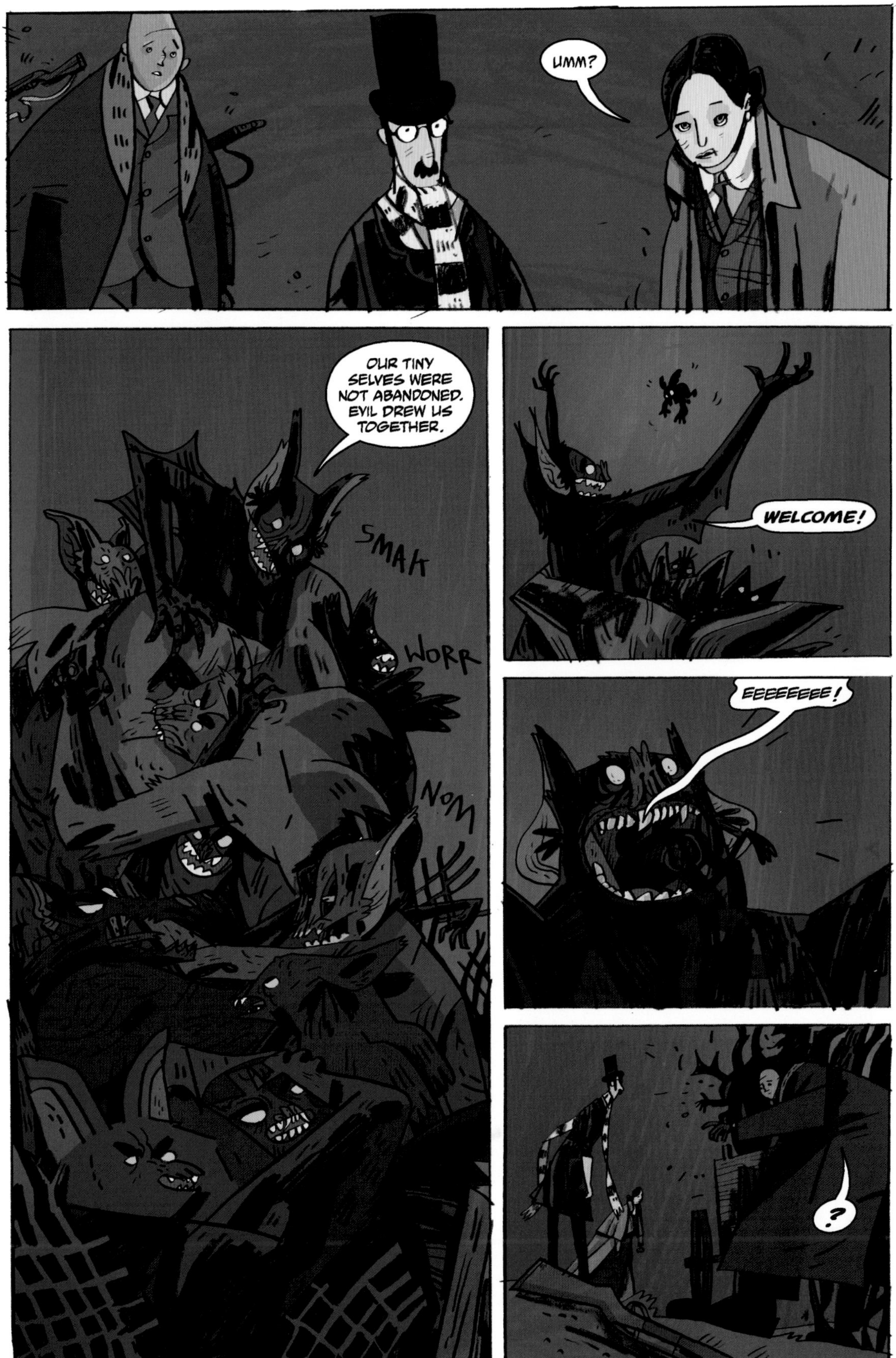
UMM?
OUR TINY SELVES WERE NOT ABANDONED. EVIL DREW US TOGETHER.
SMAK
WORR
NOM
WELCOME!
EEEEEEEE!
?

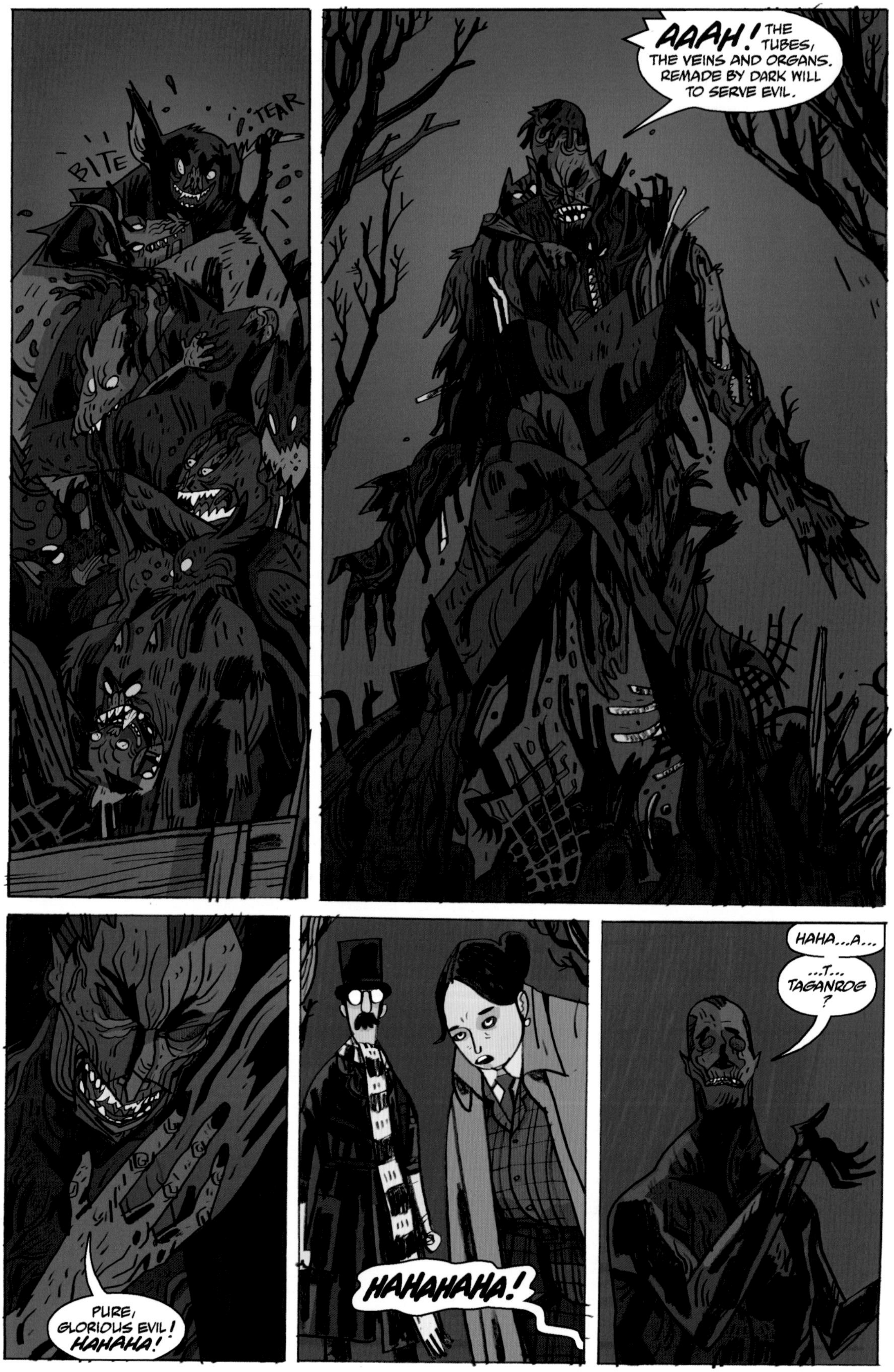
BITE
TEAR
AAAH! THE TUBES, THE VEINS AND ORGANS. REMADE BY DARK WILL TO SERVE EVIL.
PURE, GLORIOUS EVIL! HAHAHA!
HAHAHAHA!
HAHA...A...
...T... TAGANROG?

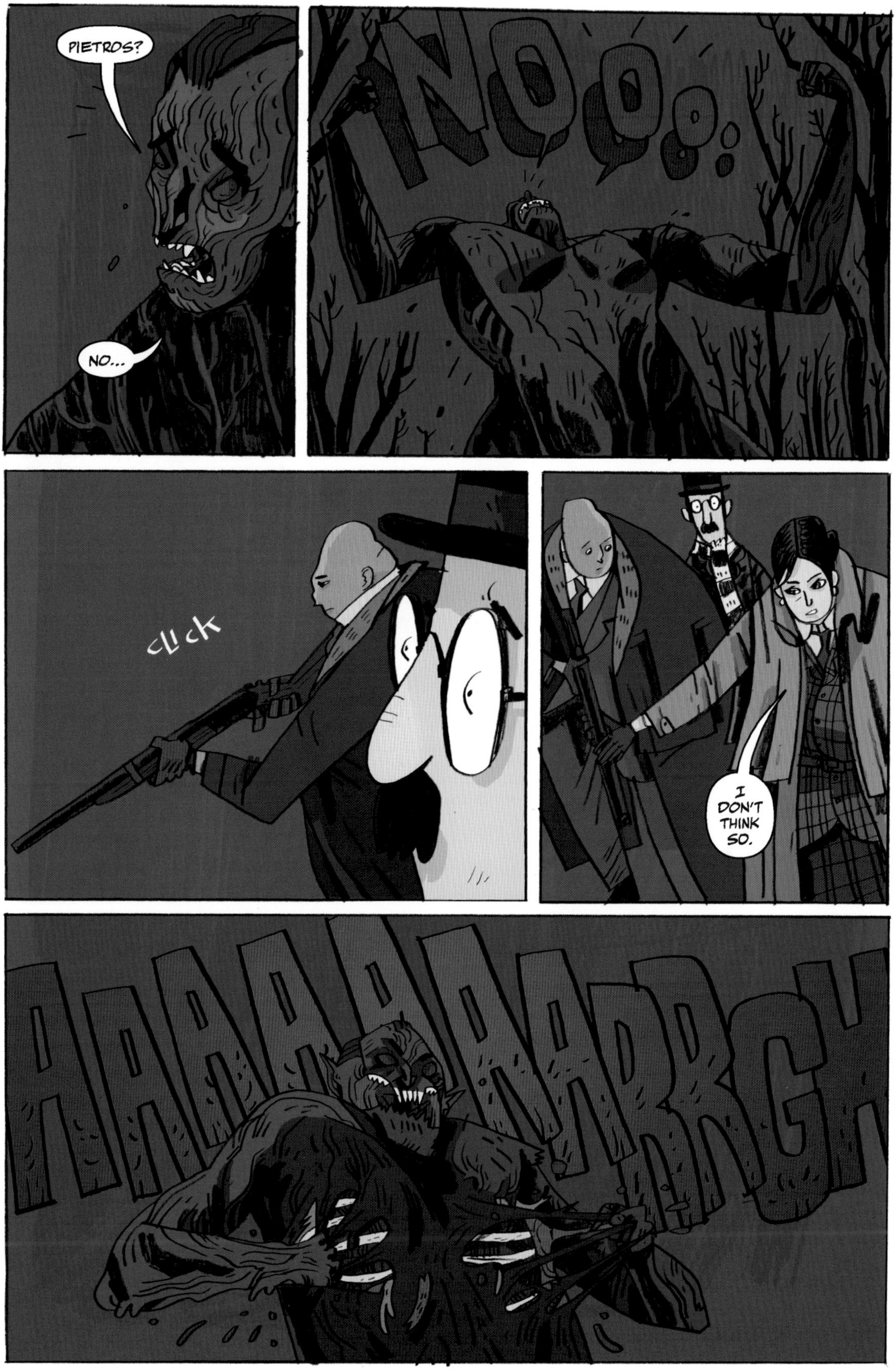
PIETROS?
NO...
NOOO...
CLICK
I DON'T THINK SO.
AAAAAAARRGH

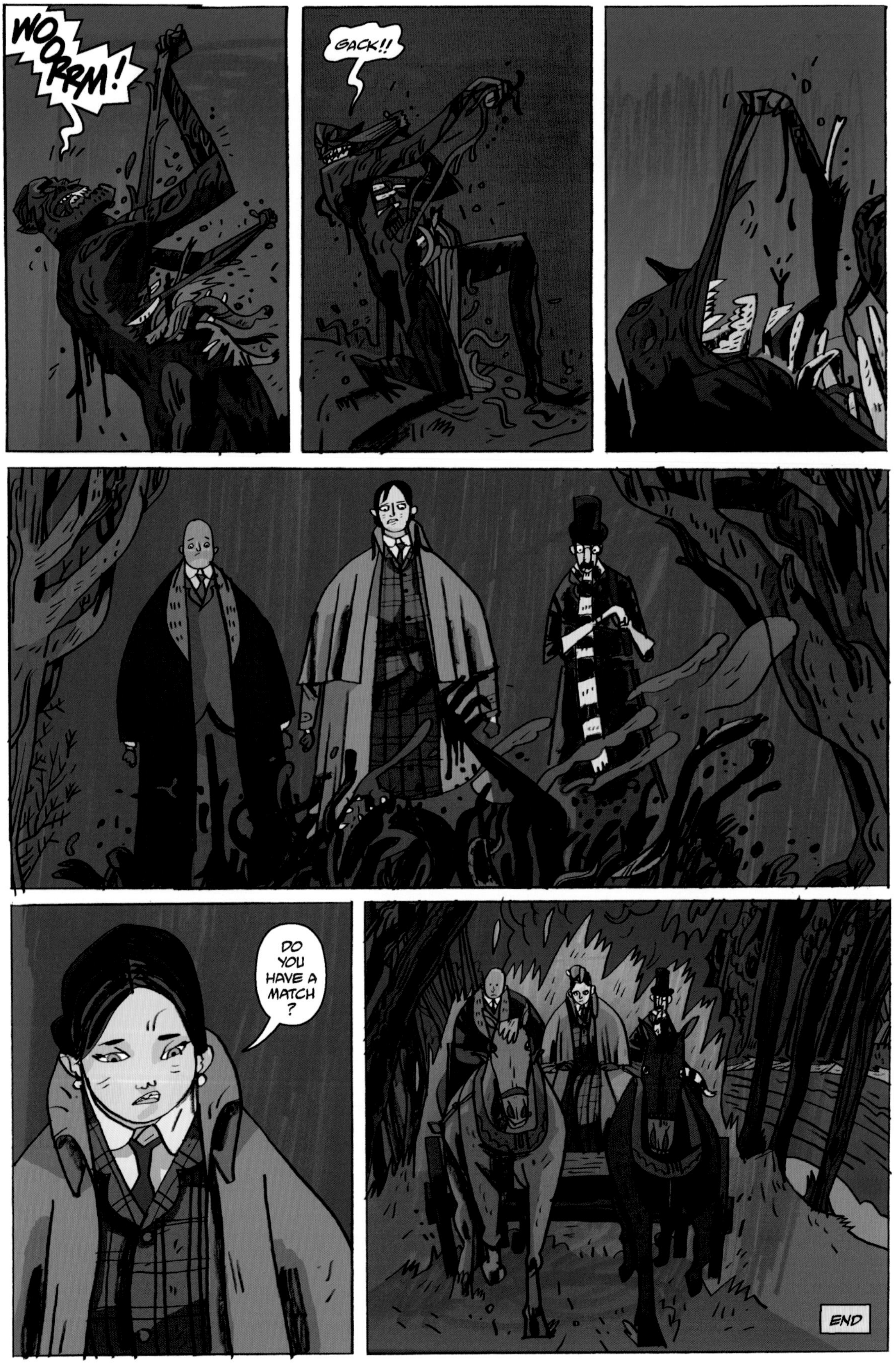
WOORRM!
GACK!!
DO YOU HAVE A MATCH?
END

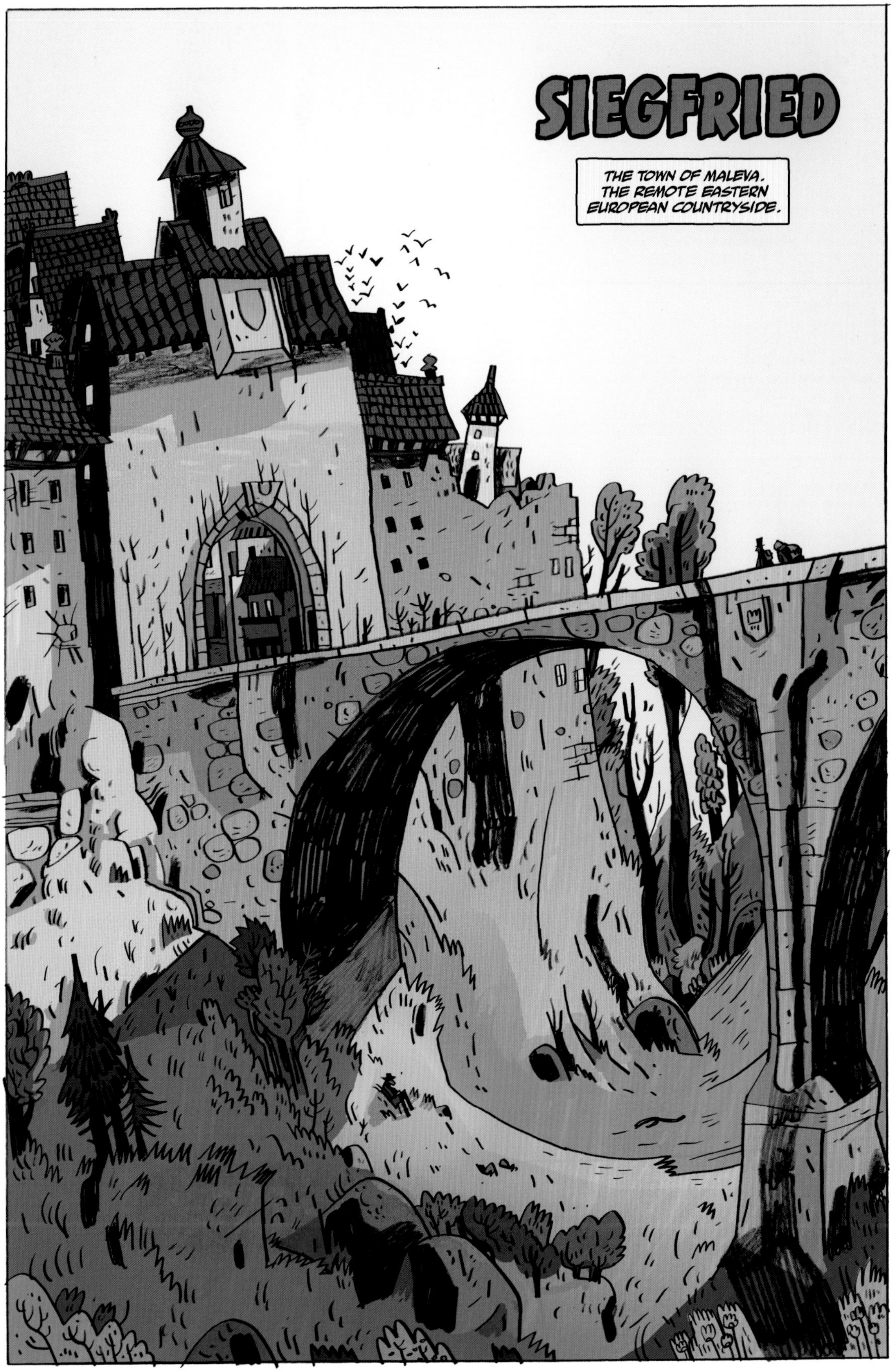
SIEGFRIED
THE TOWN OF MALEVA. THE REMOTE EASTERN EUROPEAN COUNTRYSIDE.

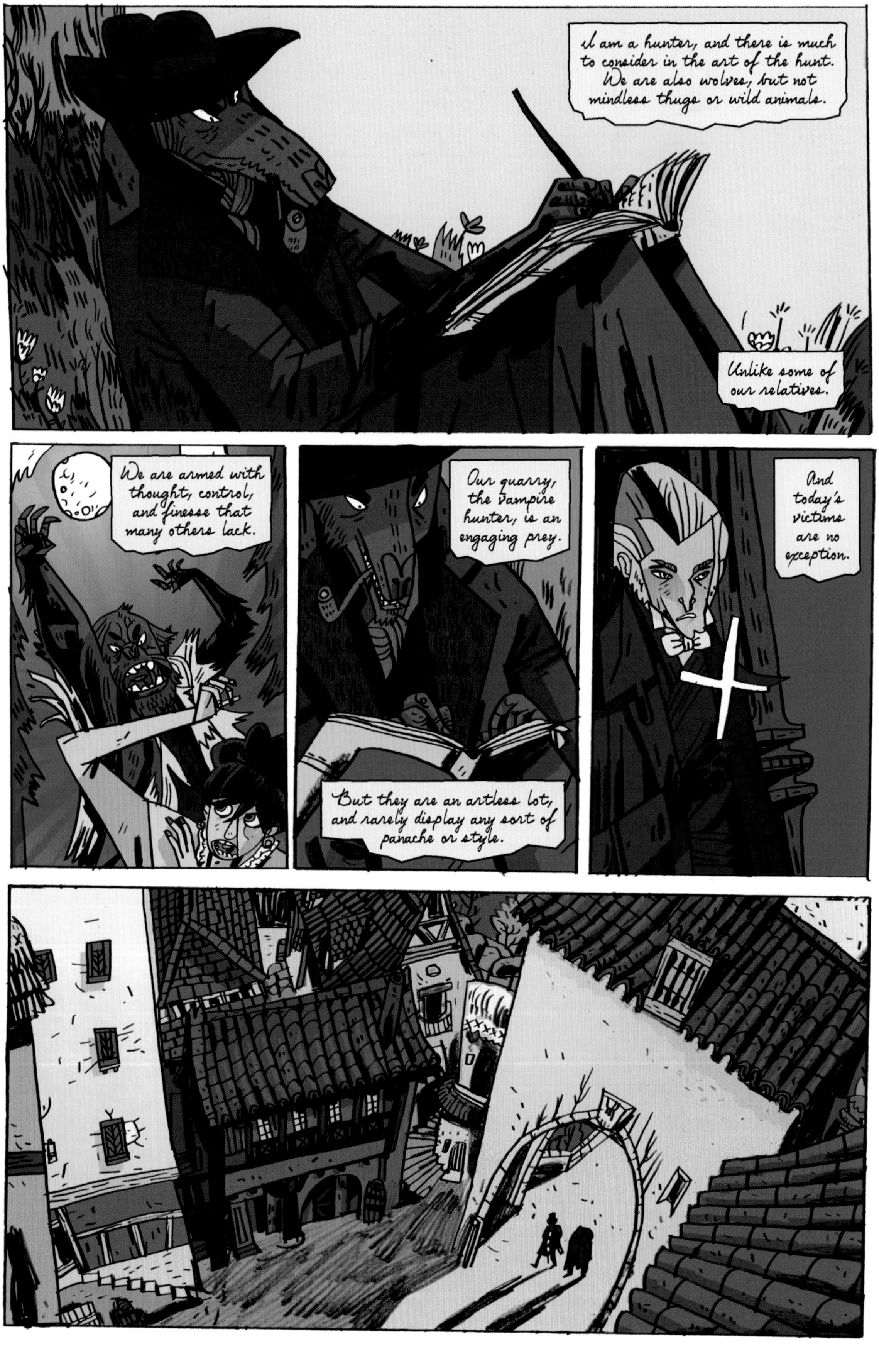
I am a hunter, and there is much to consider in the art of the hunt. We are also wolves, but not mindless thugs or wild animals.
Unlike some of our relatives.
We are armed with thought, control, and finesse that many others lack.
Our quarry, the vampire hunter, is an engaging prey.
But they are an artless lot, and rarely display any sort of panache or style.
And today's victims are no exception.

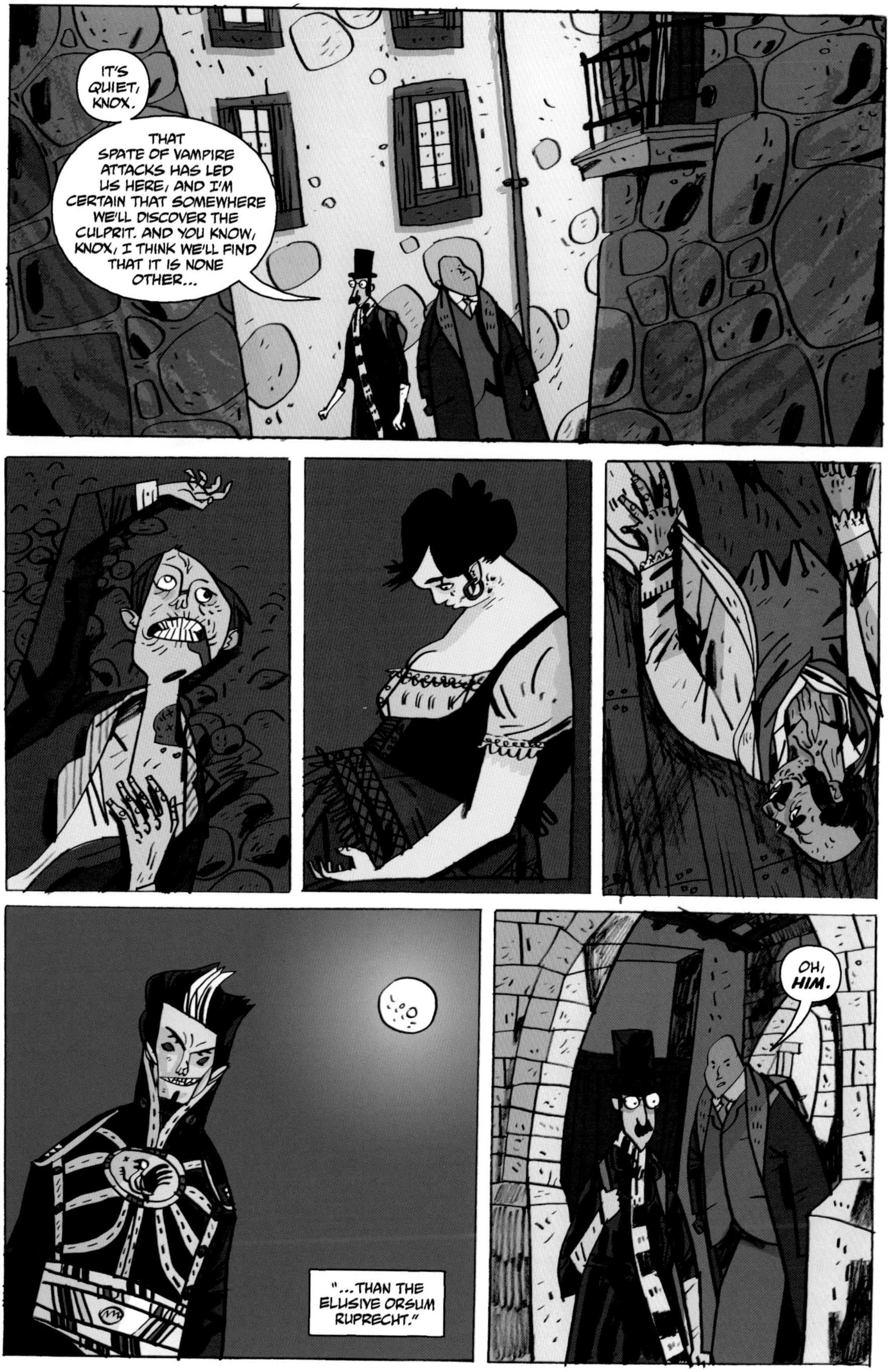
IT'S QUIET, KNOX.
THAT SPATE OF VAMPIRE ATTACKS HAS LED US HERE, AND I'M CERTAIN THAT SOMEWHERE WE'LL DISCOVER THE CULPRIT. AND YOU KNOW, KNOX, I THINK WE'LL FIND THAT IT IS NONE OTHER...
"...THAN THE ELUSIVE ORSUM RUPRECHT."
OH, **HIM.**

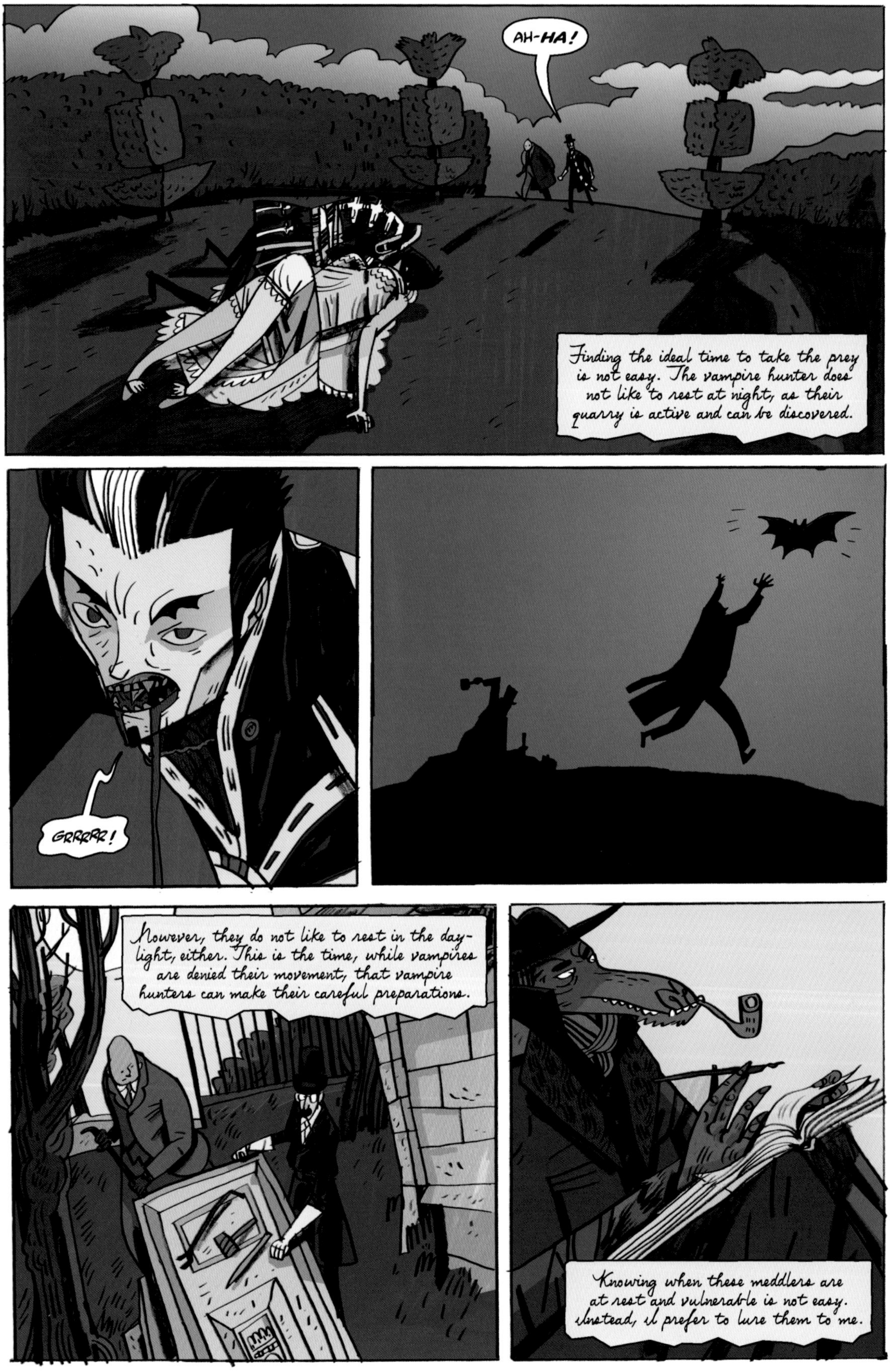
AH-HA!
Finding the ideal time to take the prey is not easy. The vampire hunter does not like to rest at night, as their quarry is active and can be discovered.
GRRRRR!
However, they do not like to rest in the daylight, either. This is the time, while vampires are denied their movement, that vampire hunters can make their careful preparations.
Knowing when these meddlers are at rest and vulnerable is not easy. Instead, I prefer to lure them to me.

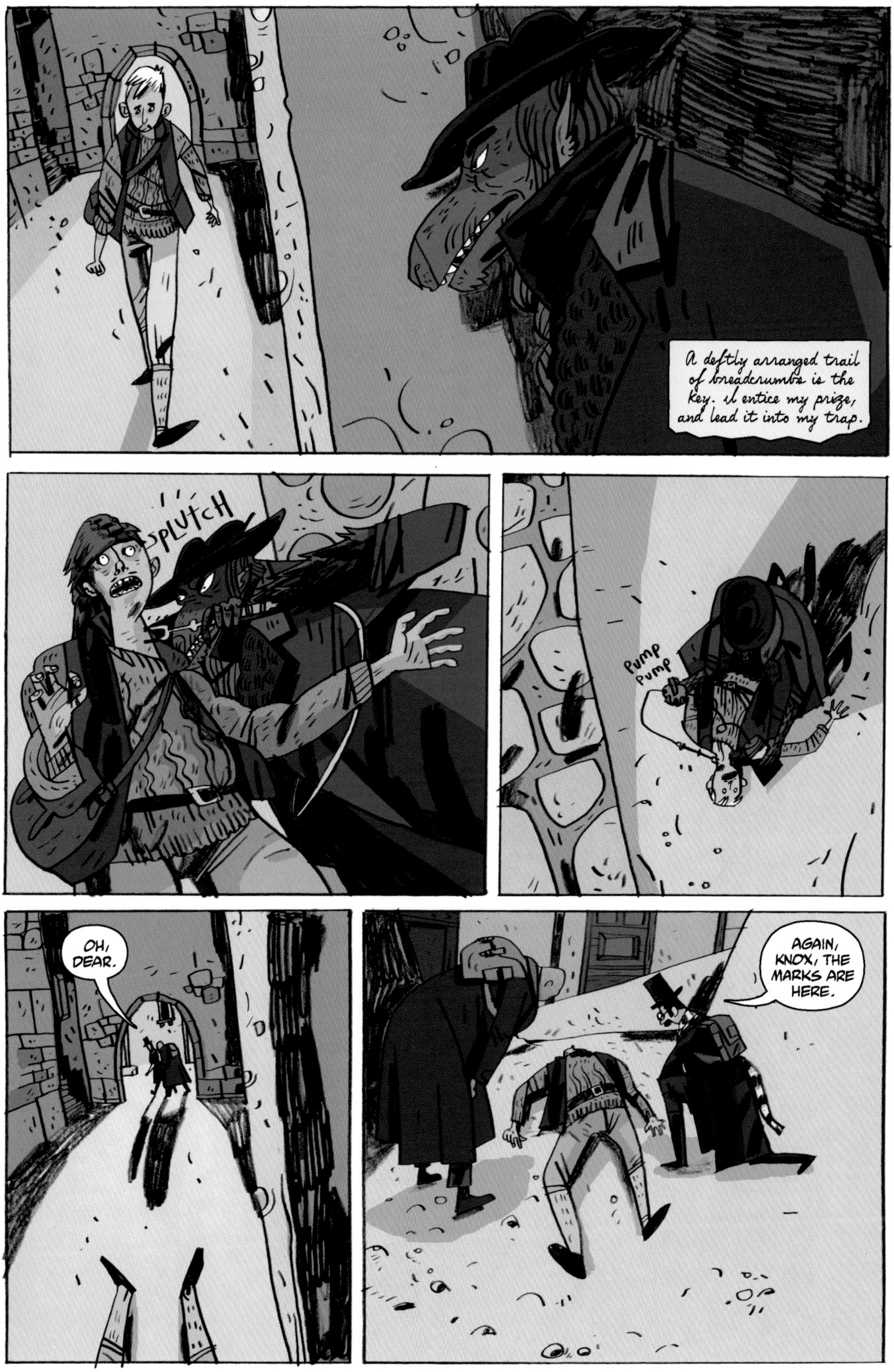
A deftly arranged trail of breadcrumbs is the key. I entice my prize, and lead it into my trap.
SPLUTCH
PUMP PUMP
OH, DEAR.
AGAIN, KNOX, THE MARKS ARE HERE.

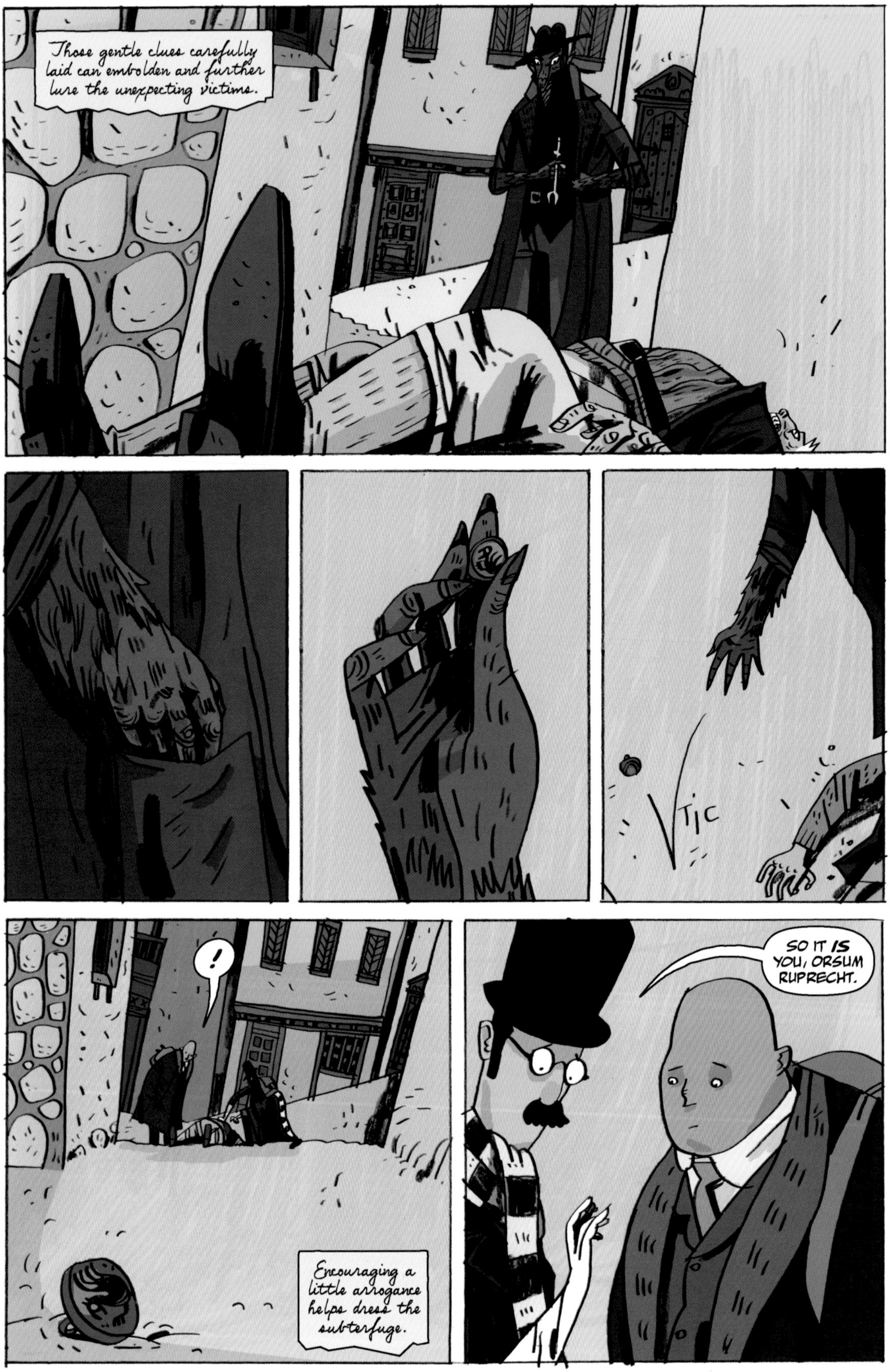
Those gentle clues carefully laid can embolden and further lure the unexpecting victims.
TIC
!
Encouraging a little arrogance helps dress the subterfuge.
SO IT IS YOU, ORSUM RUPRECHT.

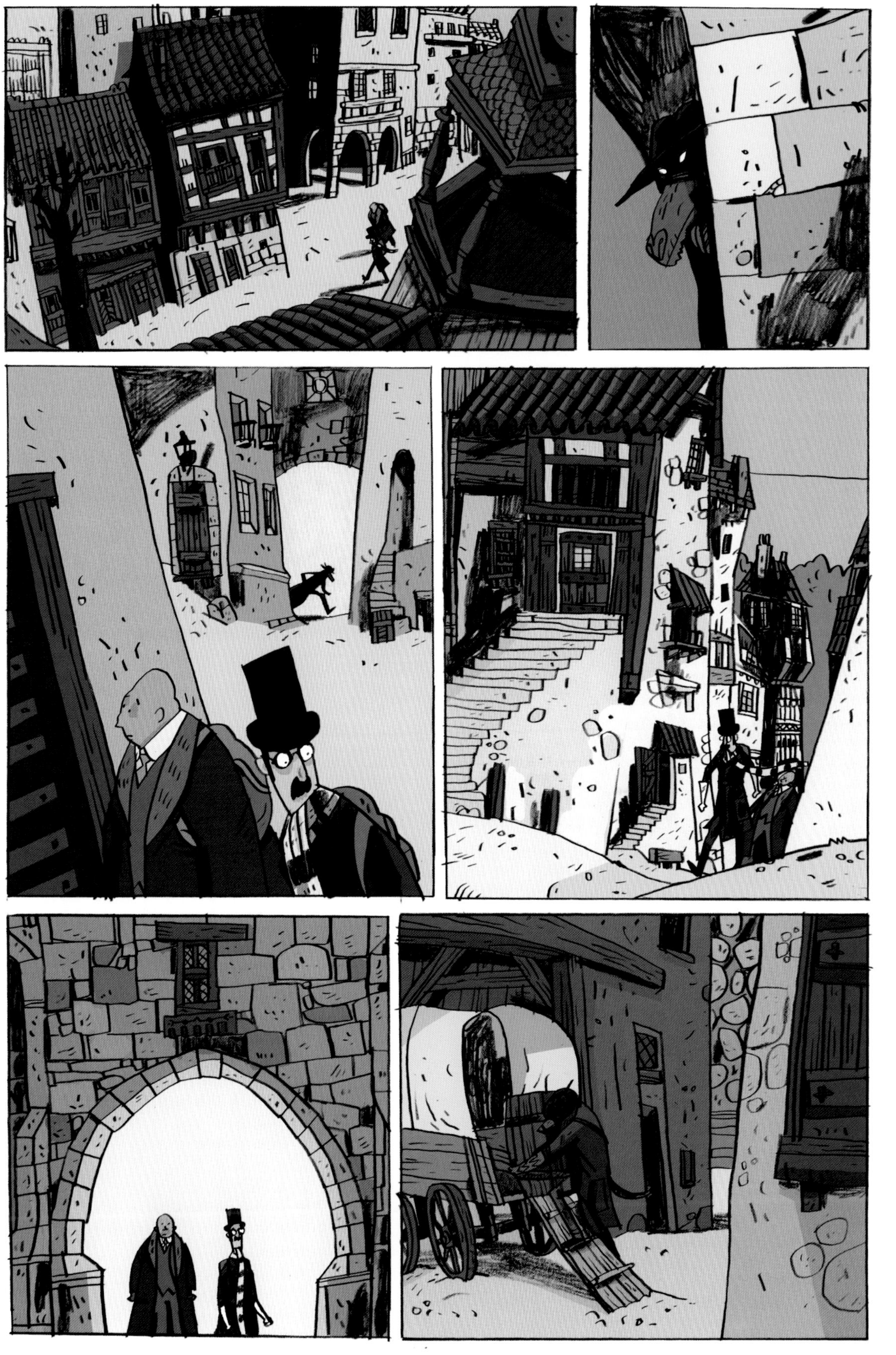

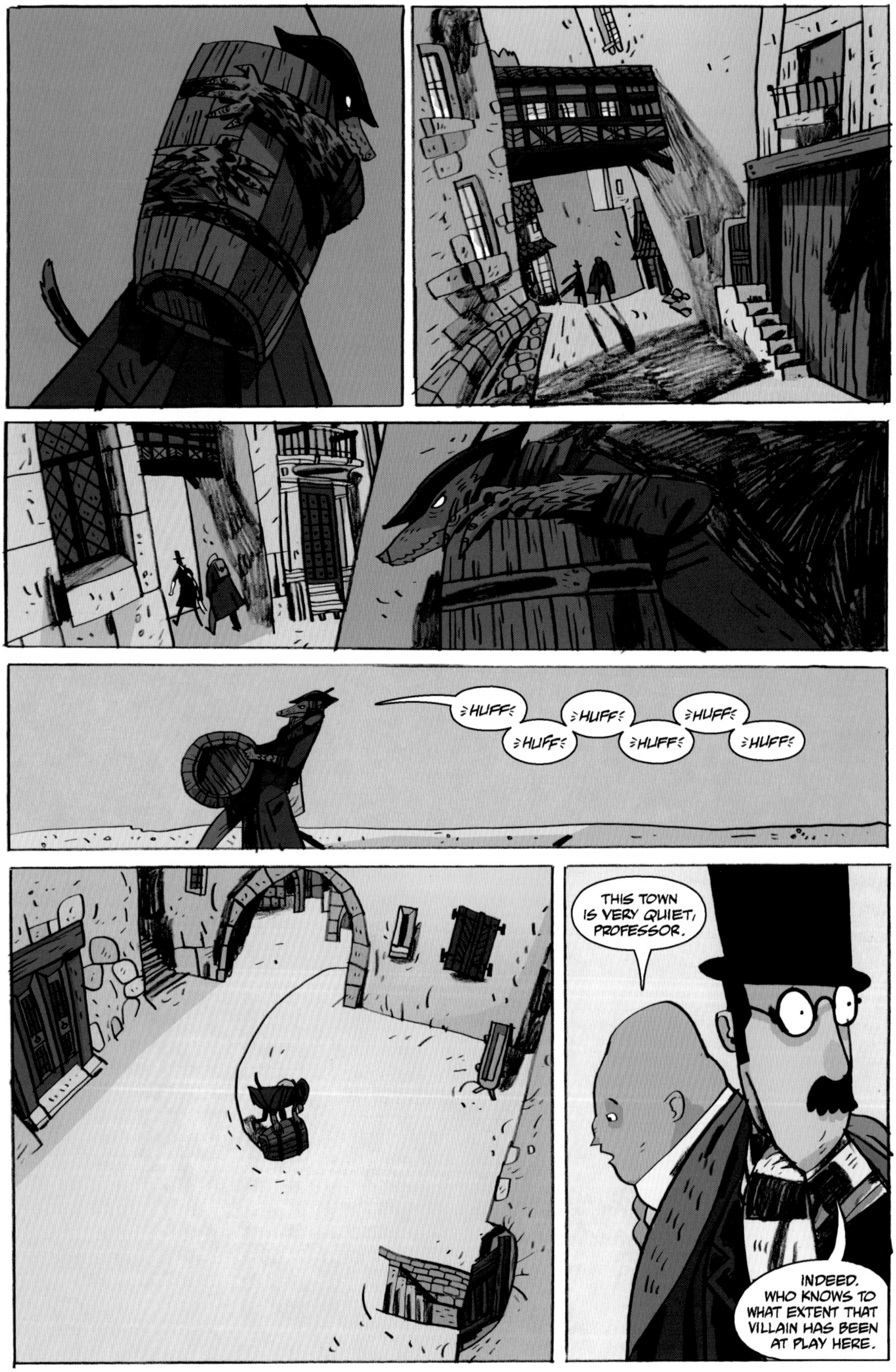
HUFF
HUFF
HUFF
HUFF
HUFF
HUFF
THIS TOWN IS VERY QUIET, PROFESSOR.
INDEED. WHO KNOWS TO WHAT EXTENT THAT VILLAIN HAS BEEN AT PLAY HERE.

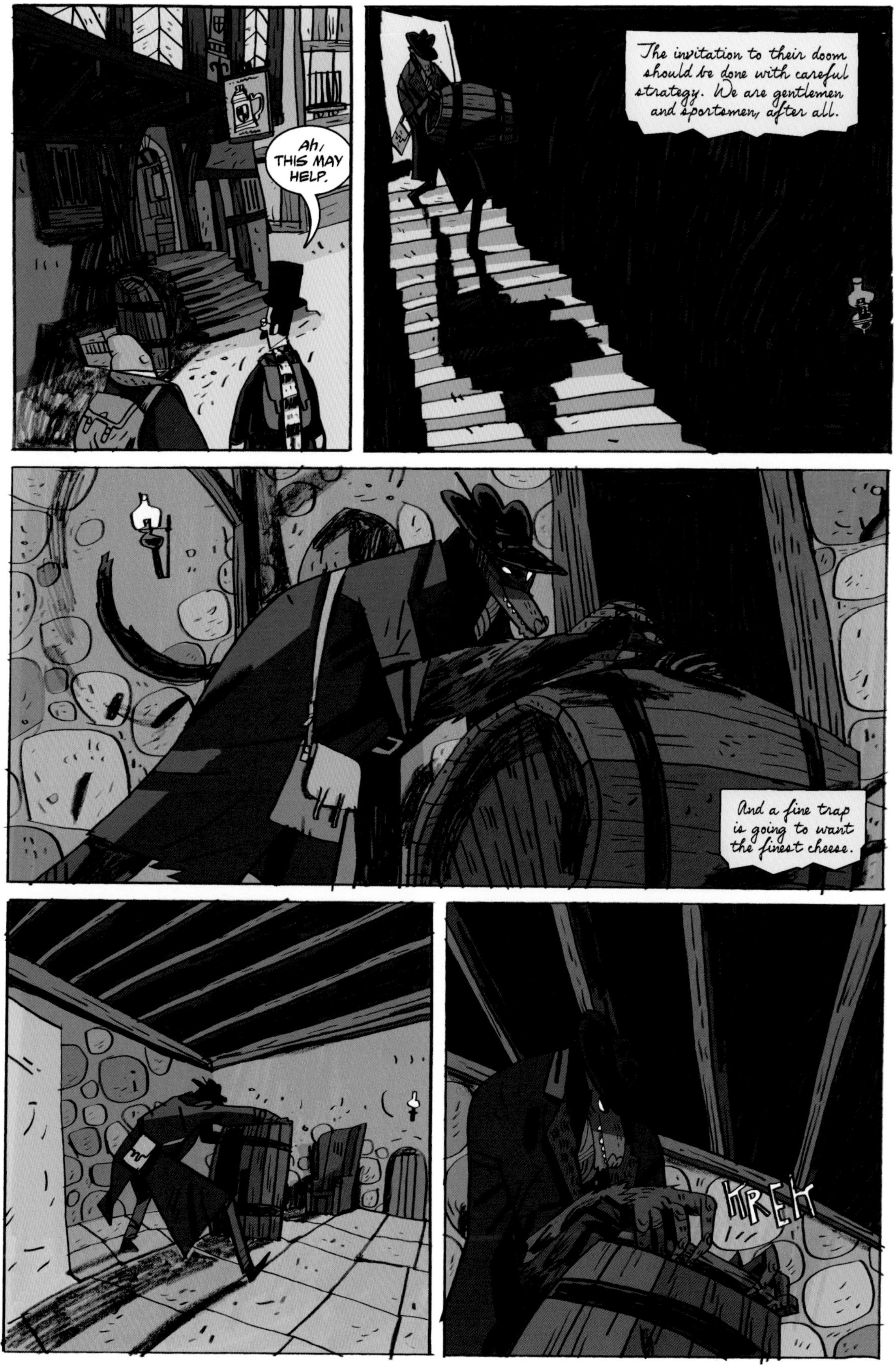
AH, THIS MAY HELP.
The invitation to their doom should be done with careful strategy. We are gentlemen and sportsmen, after all.
And a fine trap is going to want the finest cheese.
KREK

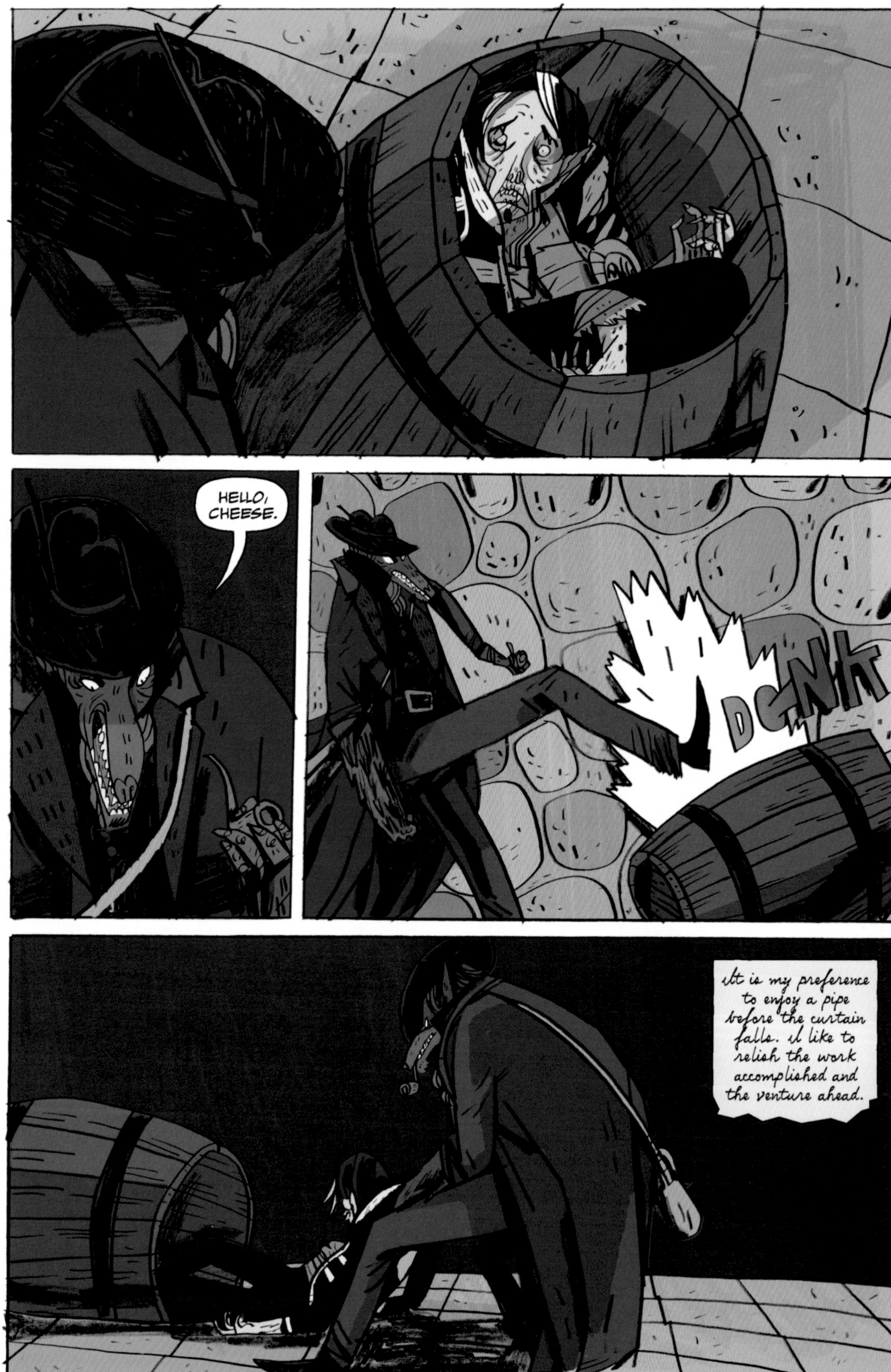
HELLO, CHEESE.
DONK
It is my preference to enjoy a pipe before the curtain falls. I like to relish the work accomplished and the venture ahead.

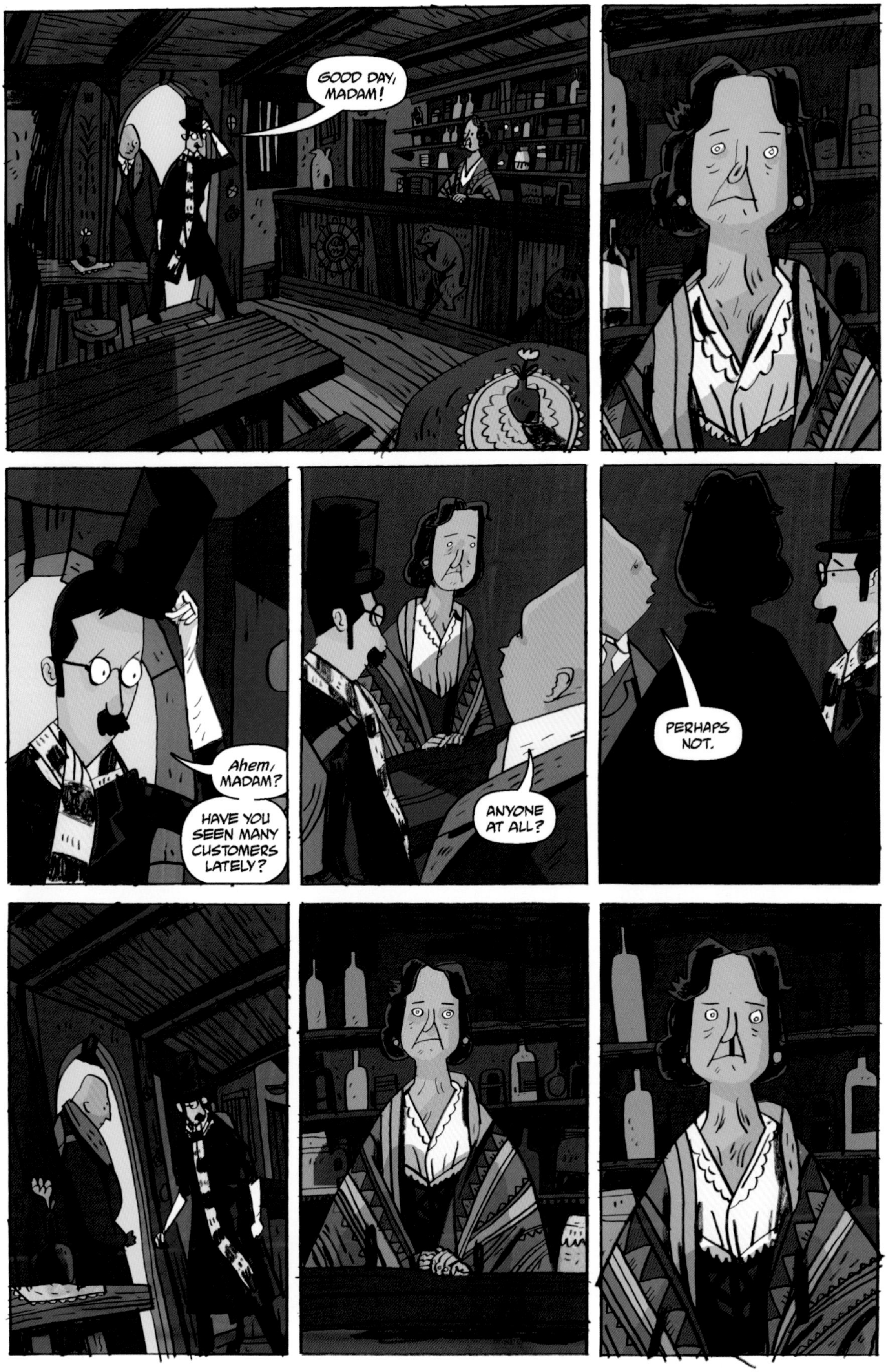
GOOD DAY, MADAM!
Ahem, MADAM?
HAVE YOU SEEN MANY CUSTOMERS LATELY?
ANYONE AT ALL?
PERHAPS NOT.

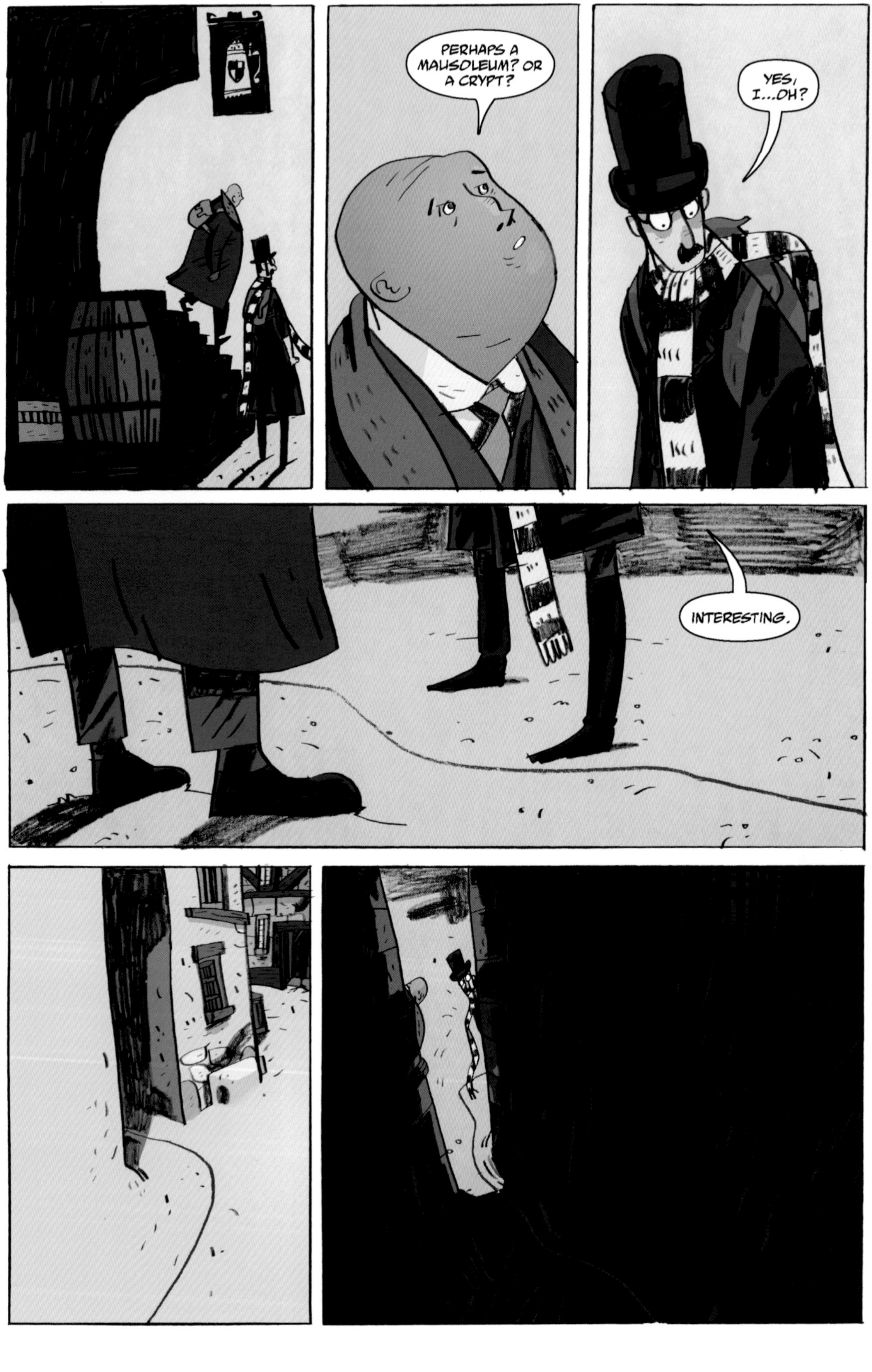
PERHAPS A MAUSOLEUM? OR A CRYPT?
YES, I...OH?
INTERESTING.

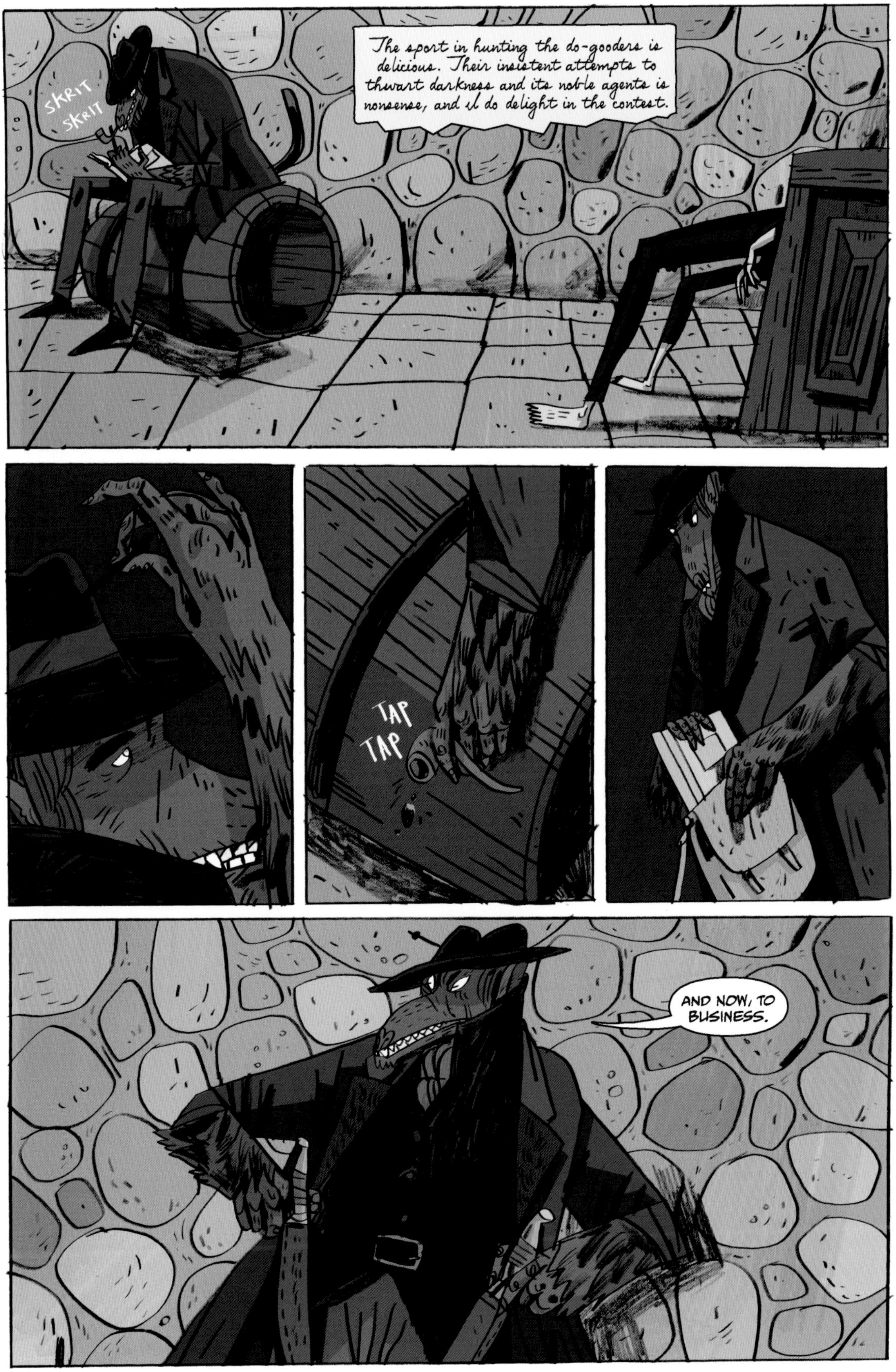
SKRIT SKRIT
The sport in hunting the do-gooders is delicious. Their insistent attempts to thwart darkness and its noble agents is nonsense, and I do delight in the contest.
TAP TAP
AND NOW, TO BUSINESS.

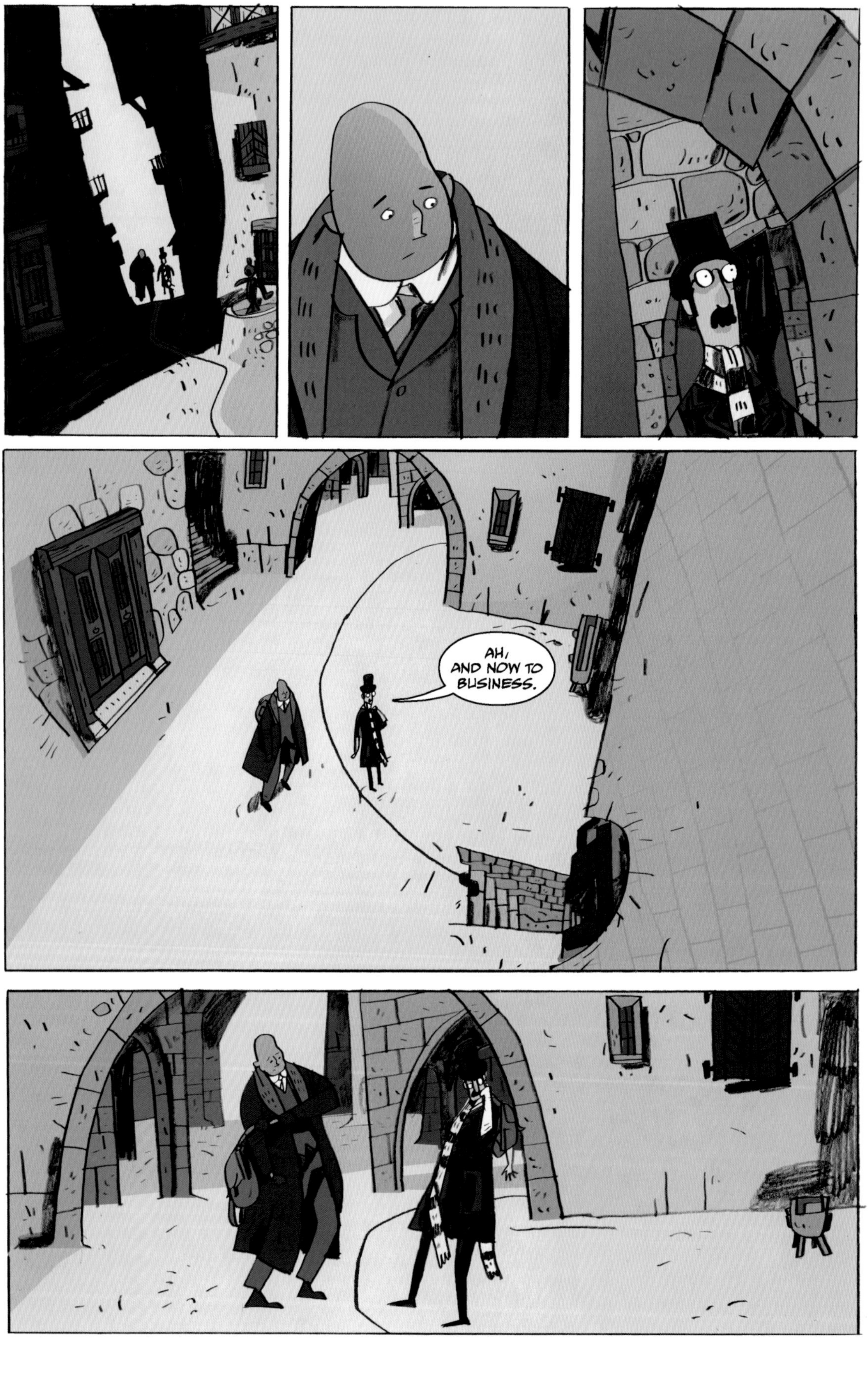
AH, AND NOW TO BUSINESS.

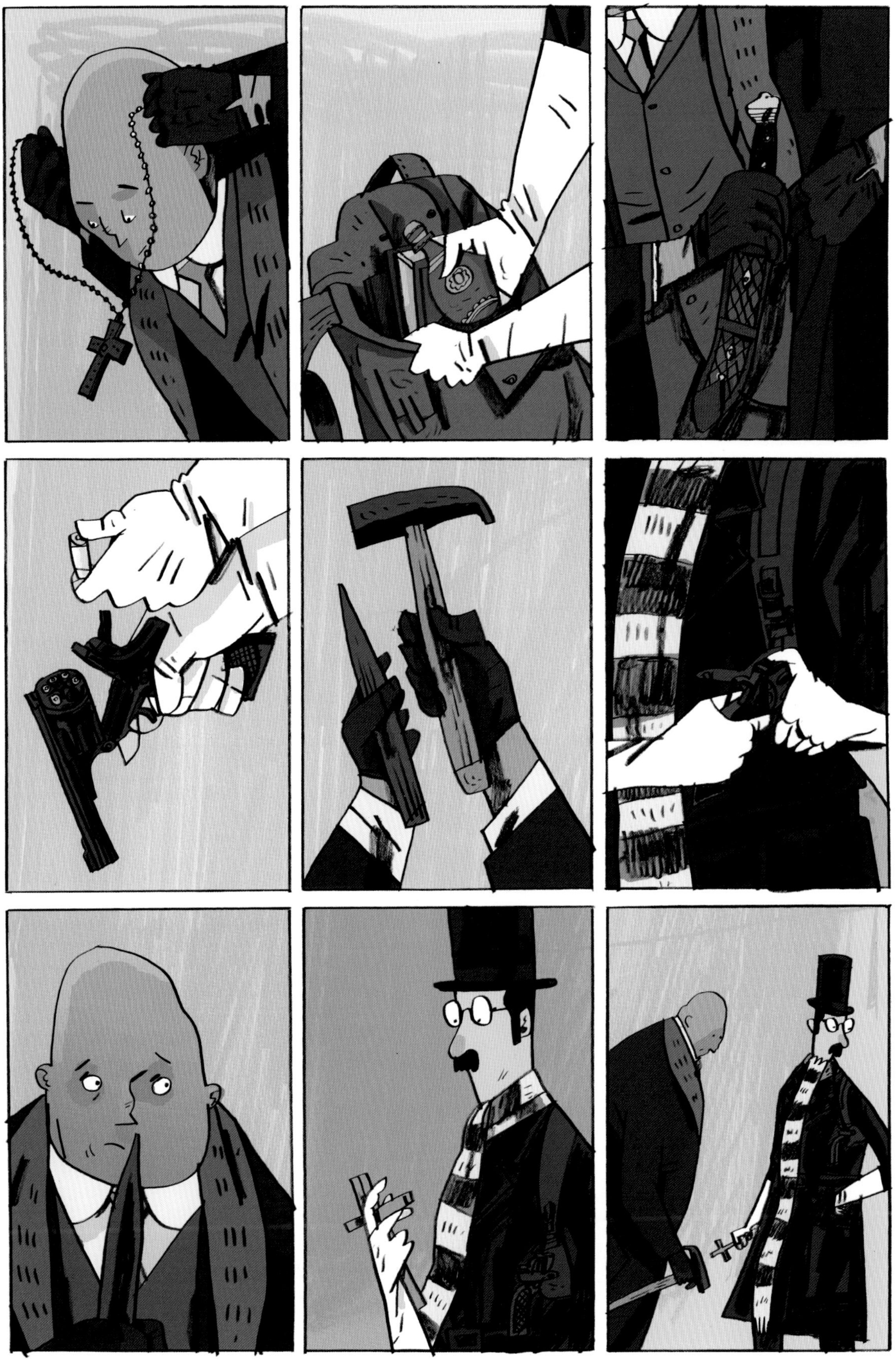

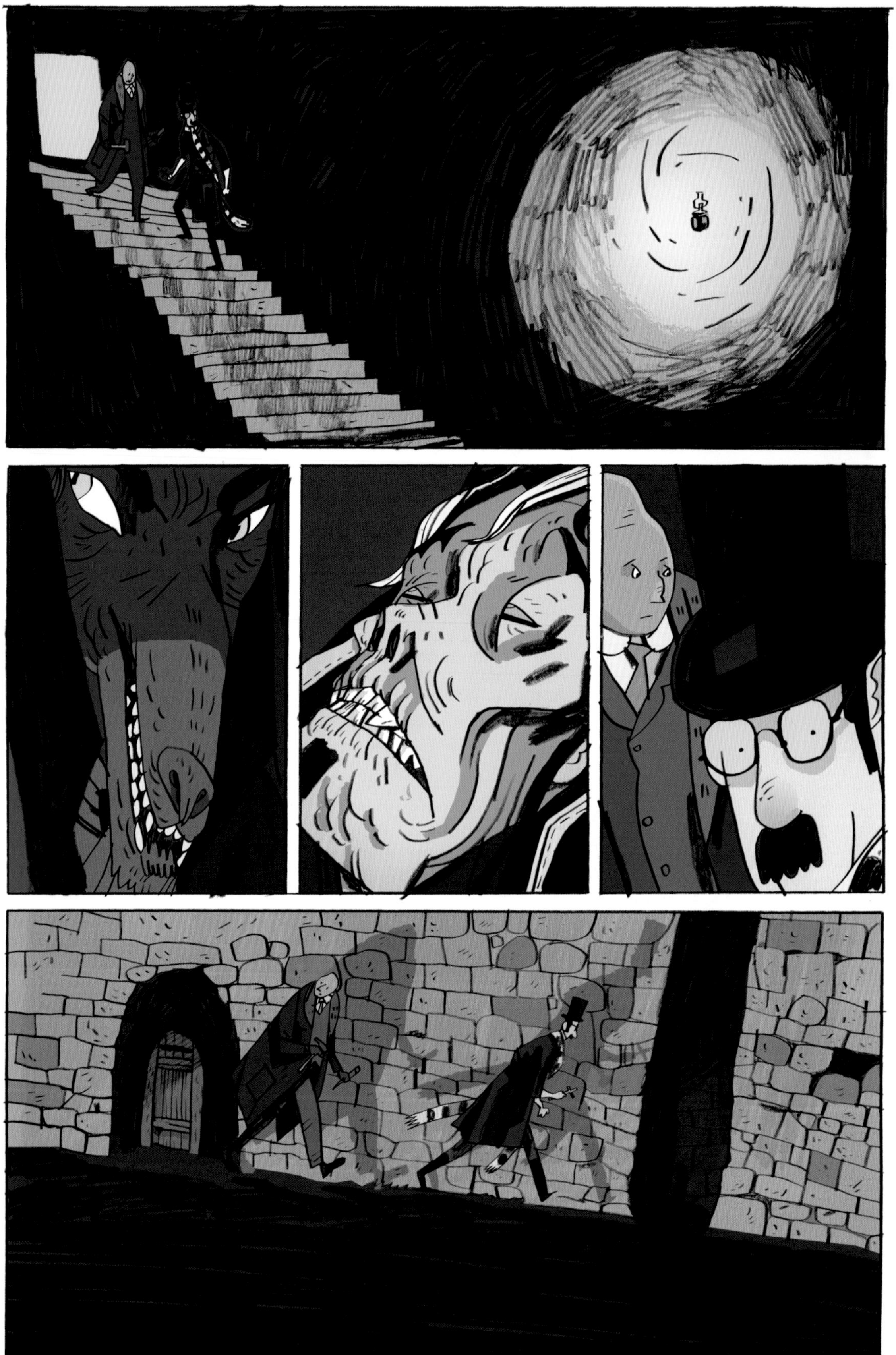

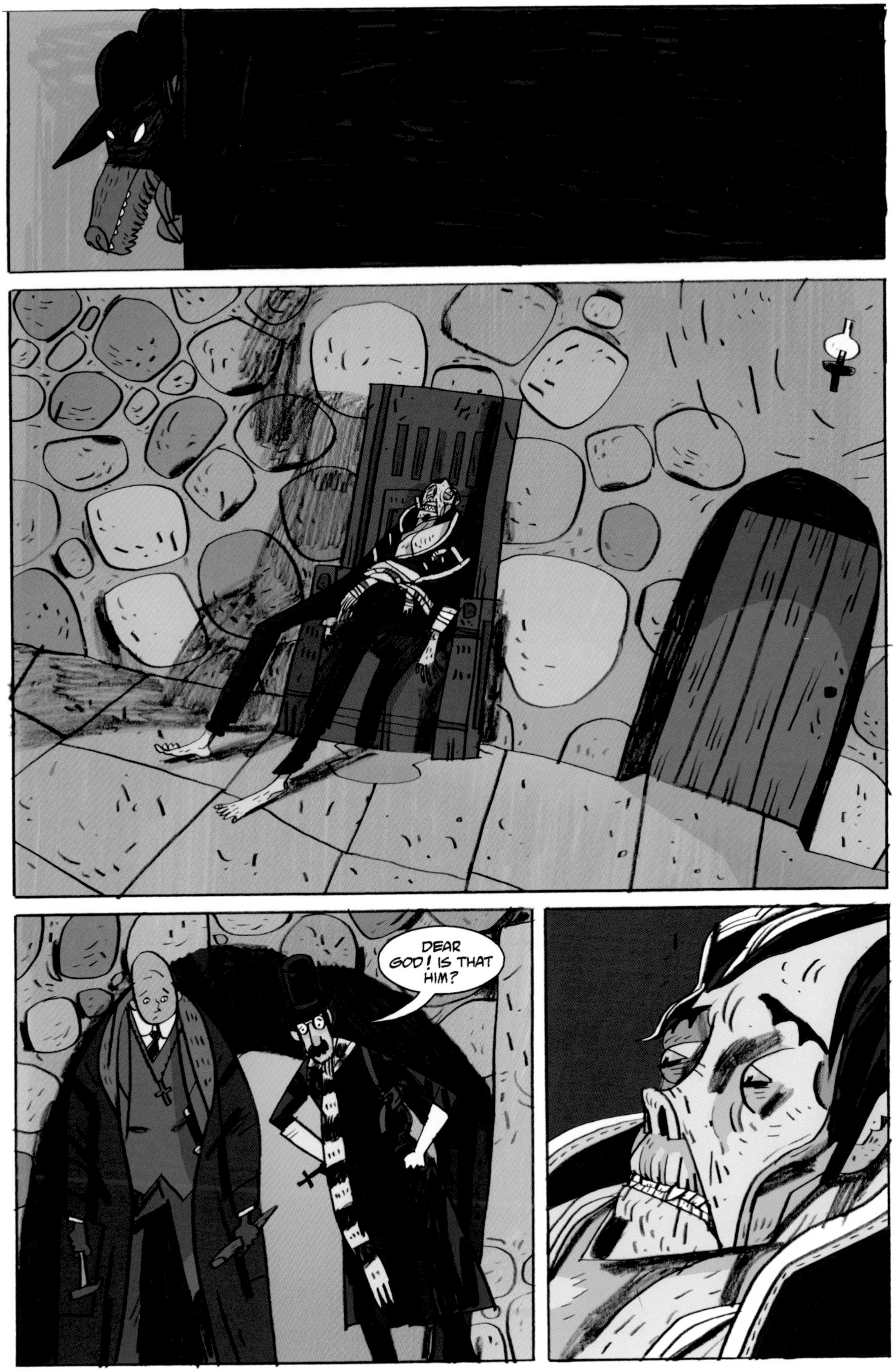
DEAR GOD! IS THAT HIM?

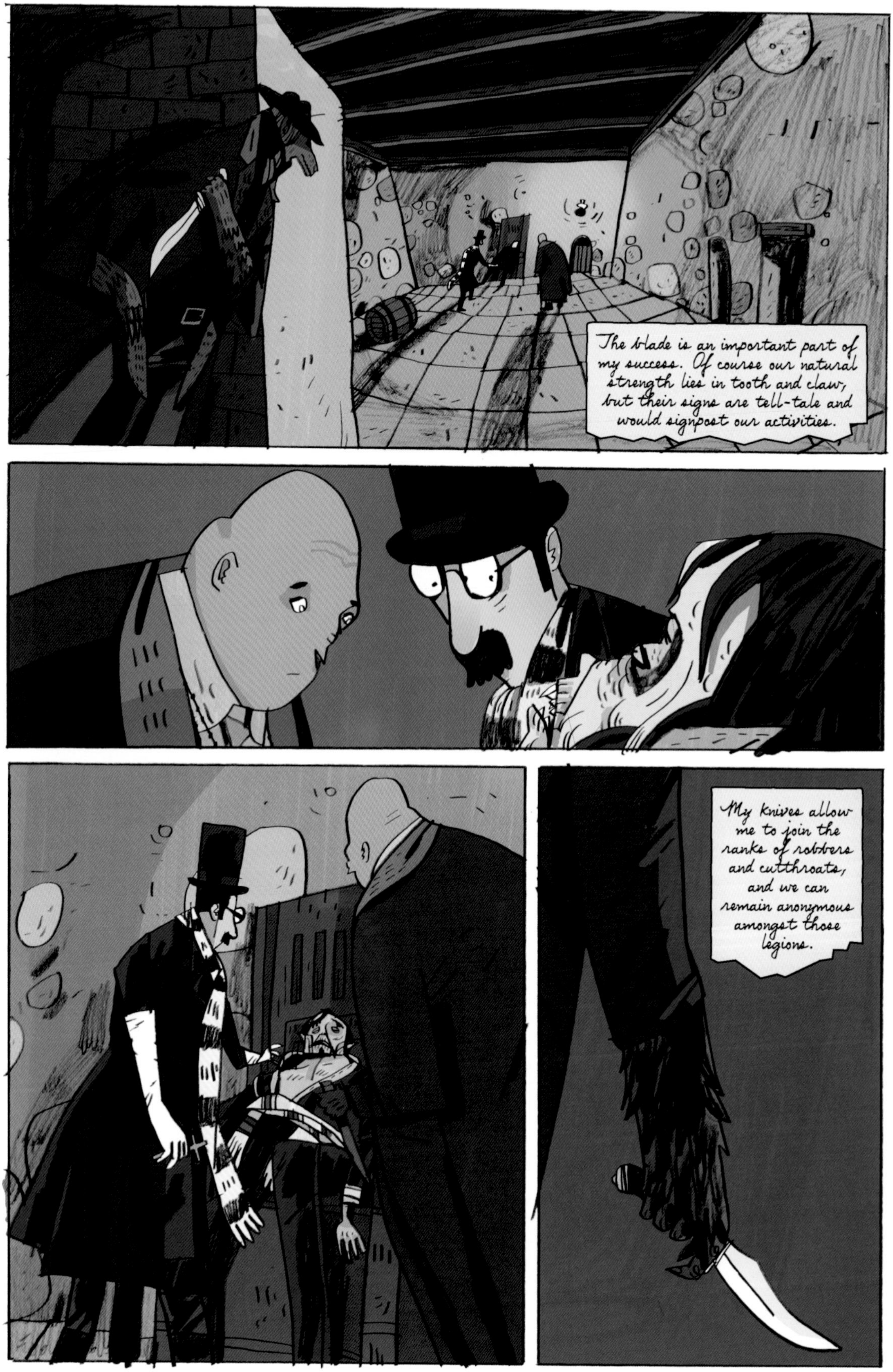
The blade is an important part of my success. Of course our natural strength lies in tooth and claw, but their signs are tell-tale and would signpost our activities.
My knives allow me to join the ranks of robbers and cutthroats, and we can remain anonymous amongst those legions.

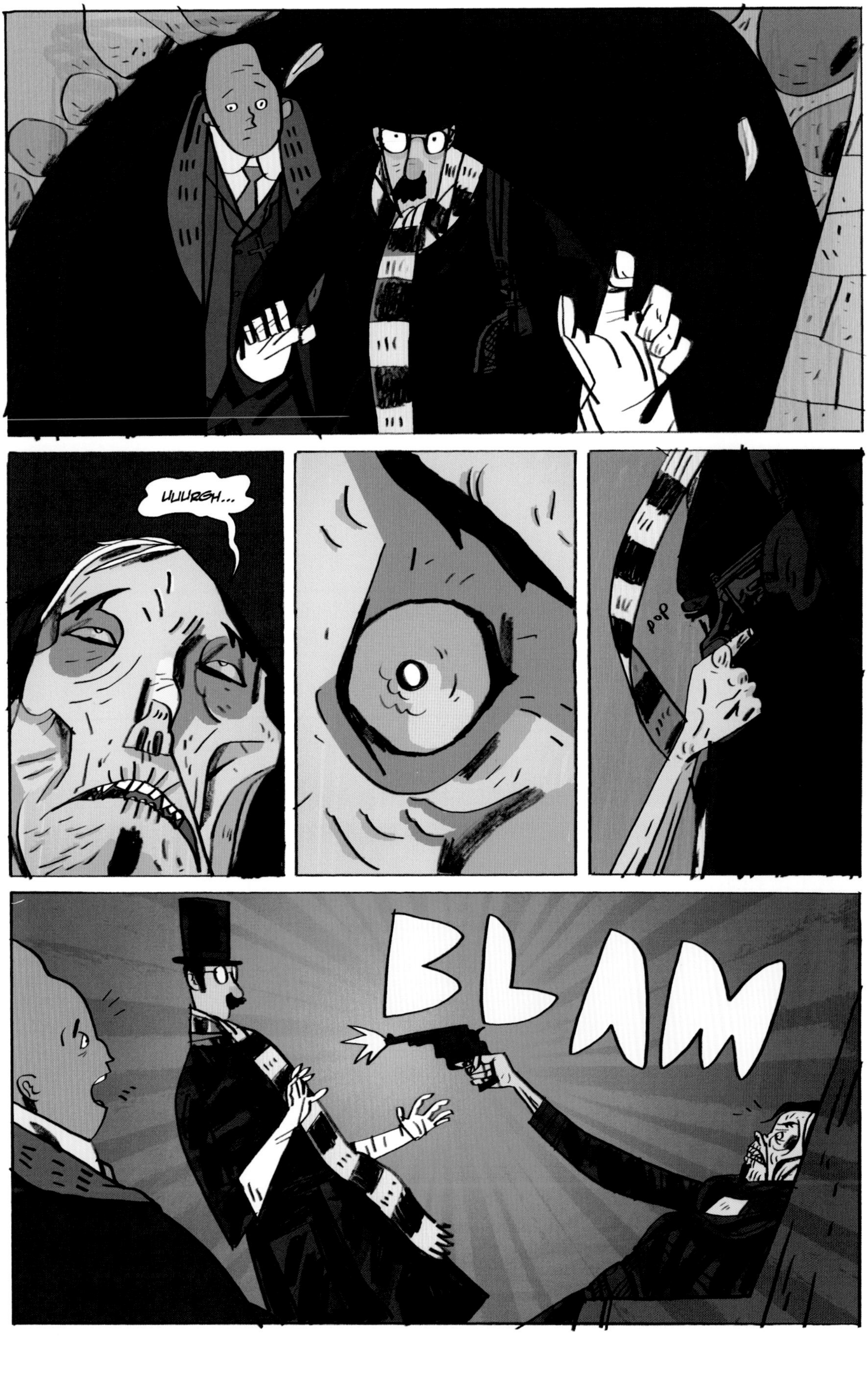
UUURGH...
pop
BLAM

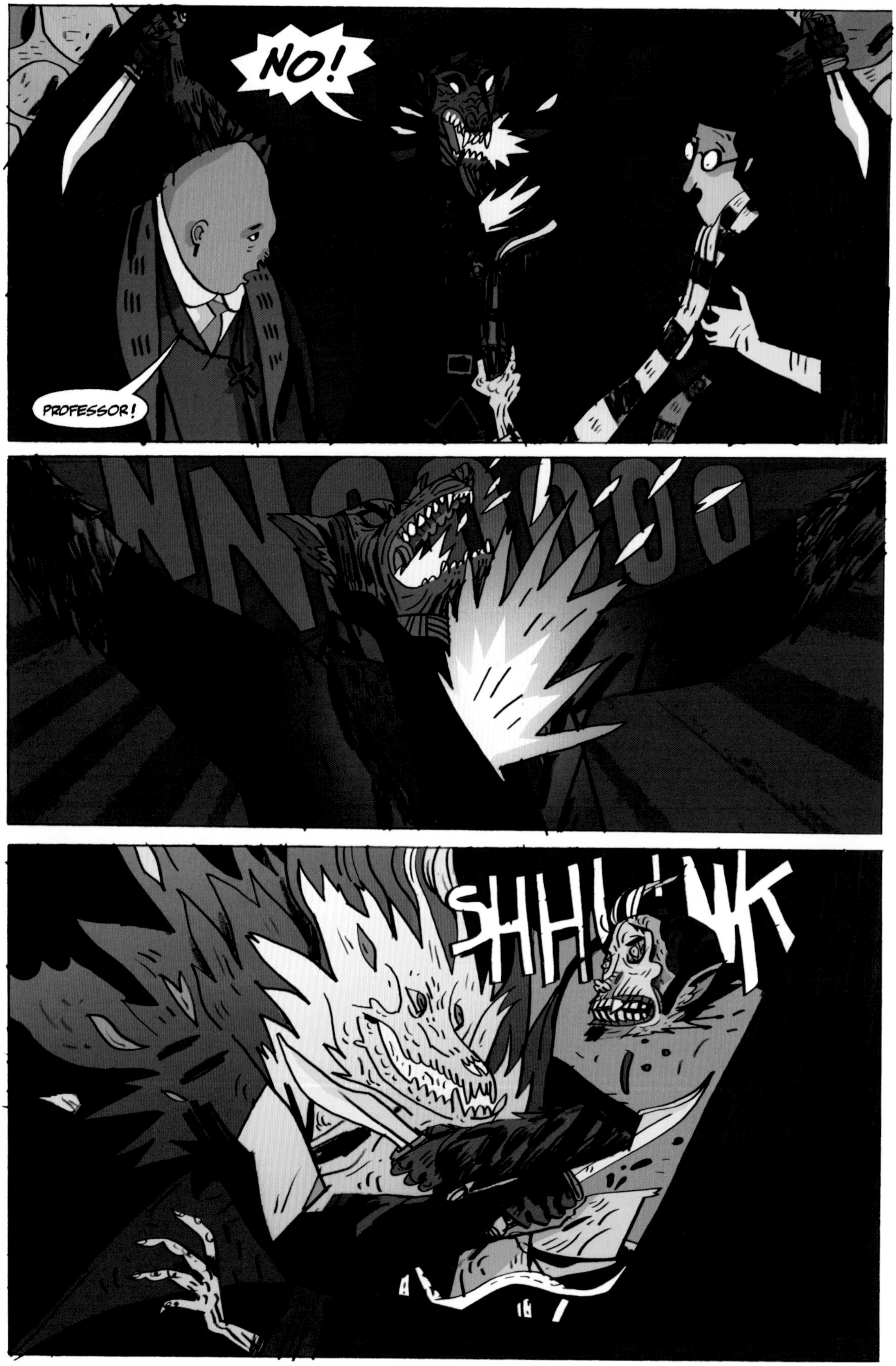
NO!
PROFESSOR!

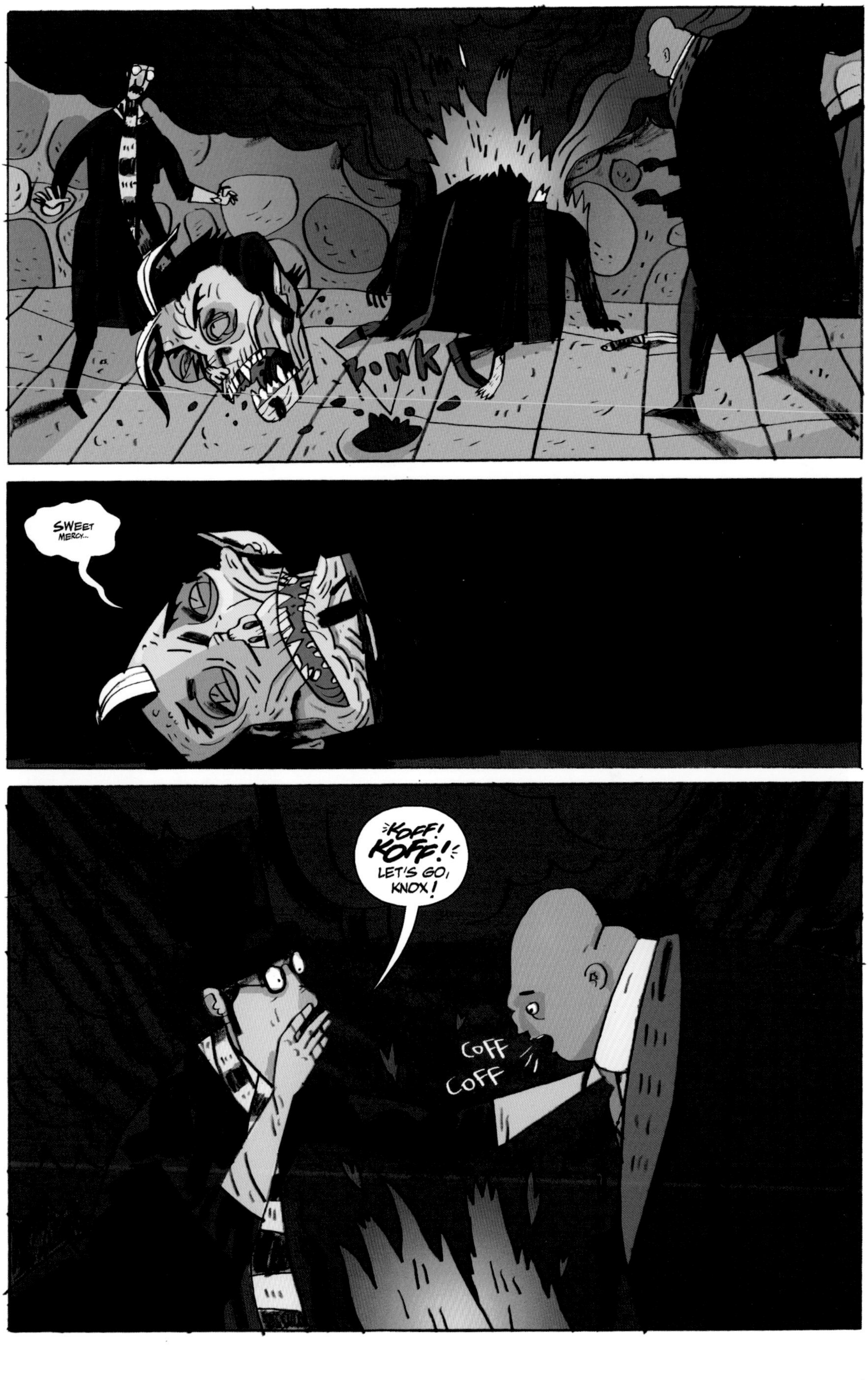
BONK
SWEET MERCY...
KOFF! KOFF! LET'S GO, KNOX!
COFF COFF

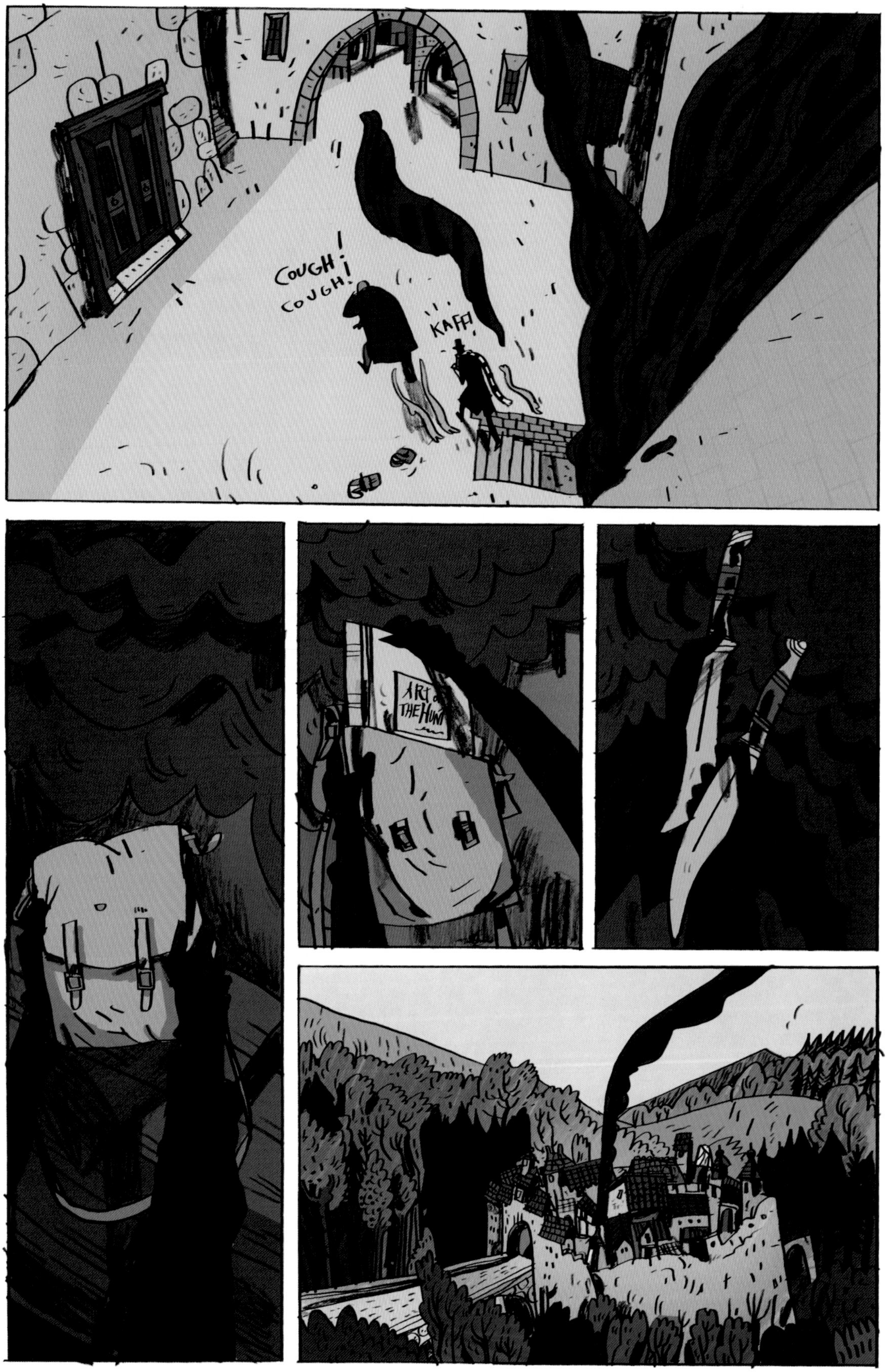
COUGH!
COUGH!
KAFF!
ART
THE HUNT

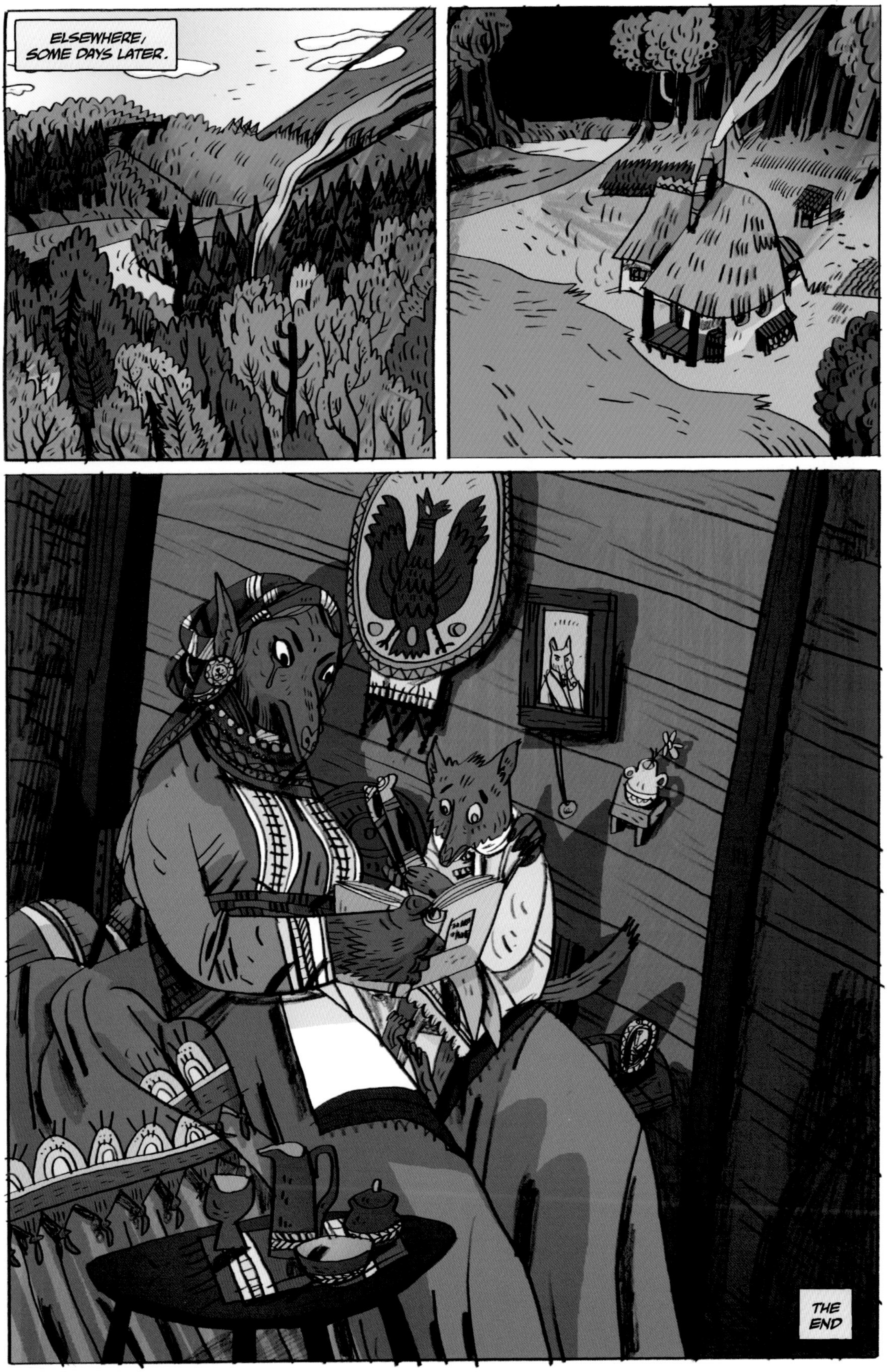
ELSEWHERE, SOME DAYS LATER.
THE END

EPILOGUE

PWEEEE EE EE EEEE

PWEEE E EE EEEE

OH!

FALCONSPEARE.

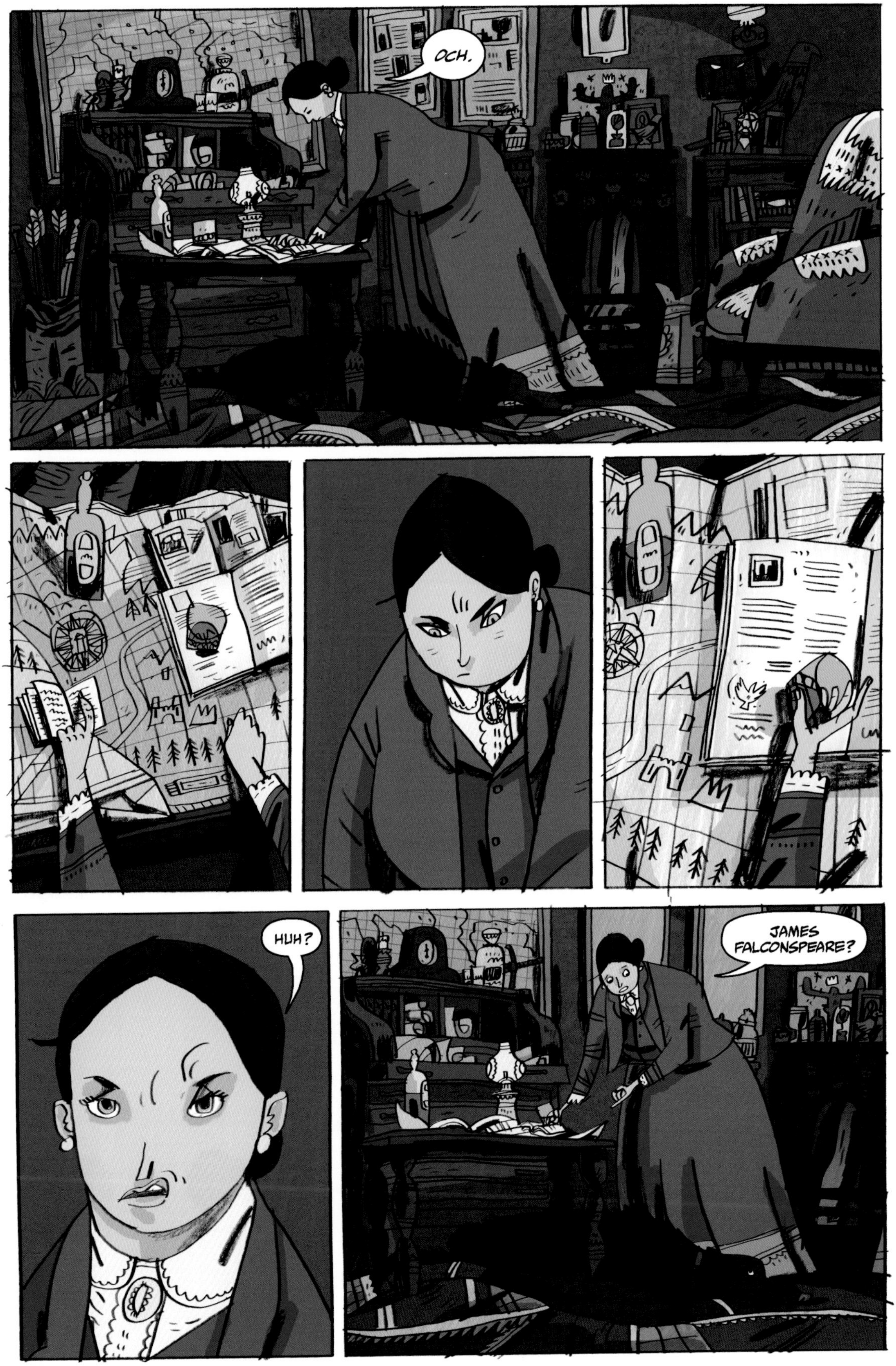
OCH.
HUH?
JAMES FALCONSPEARE?

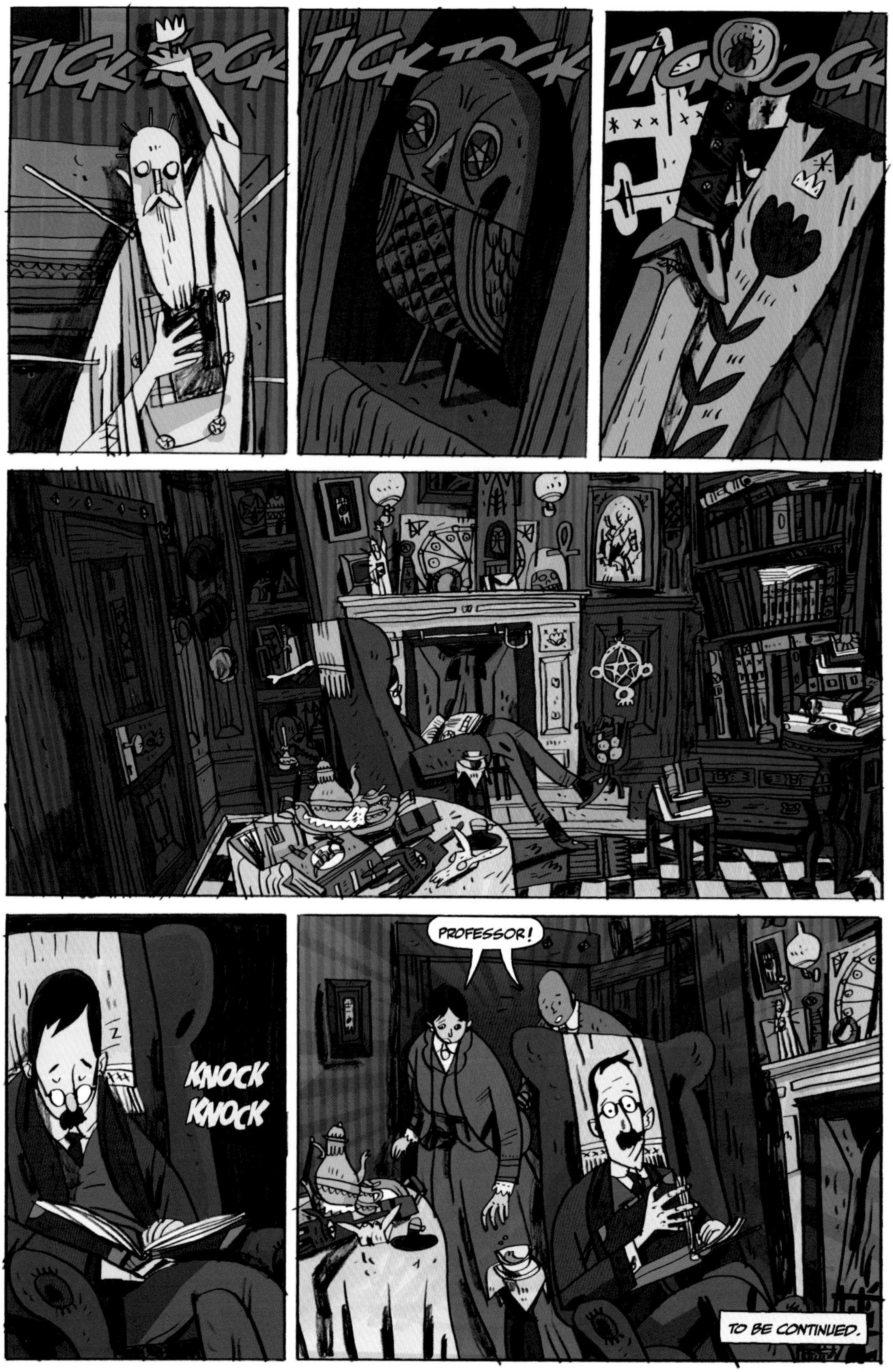
TICK TOCK
TICK TOCK
TICK TOCK
KNOCK KNOCK
PROFESSOR!
TO BE CONTINUED.

OUR ENCOUNTERS WITH EVIL

ADVENTURES OF PROFESSOR J.T. MEINHARDT
AND HIS ASSISTANT MR. KNOX

SKETCHBOOK

Notes by Warwick Johnson-Cadwell

Drawing up a cast of characters to bring to meet the Professor and Mr. Knox was great fun to do. Ms. Mary Van Sloan was a late arrival to these stories, but she has become an important part of the dynamic of these vampire hunters.

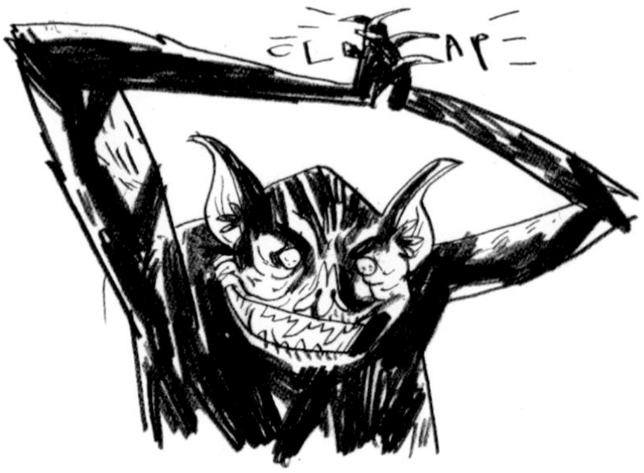

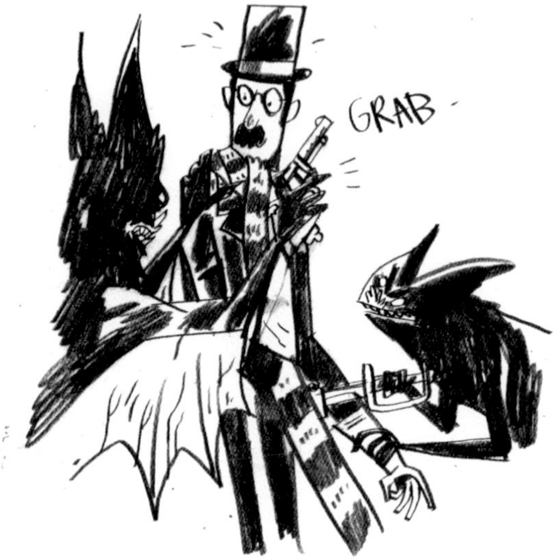
GRAB

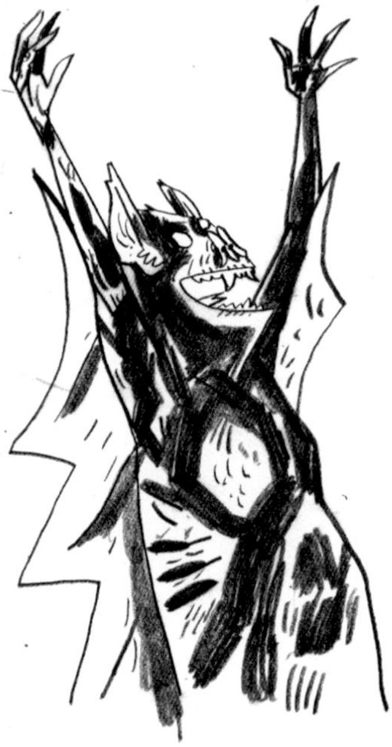

There's a world of monsters these guys can meet, as well as all the great characters that dwell in this Gothic world.

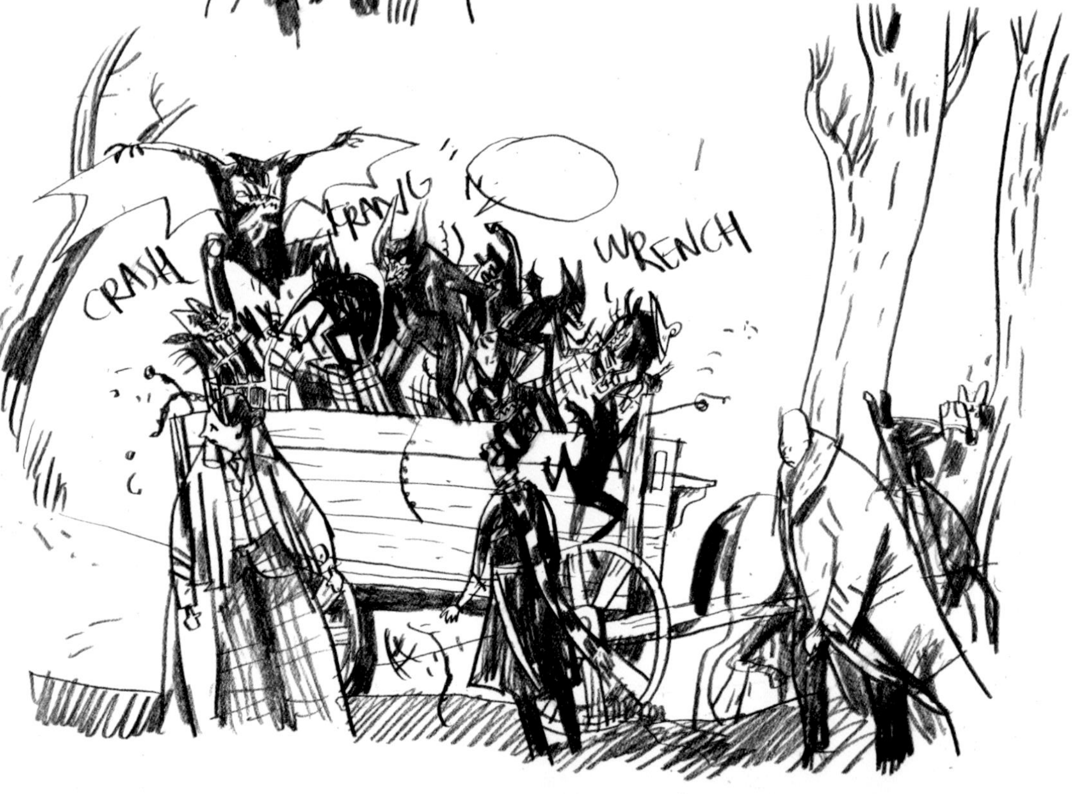
CRASH
WRENCH

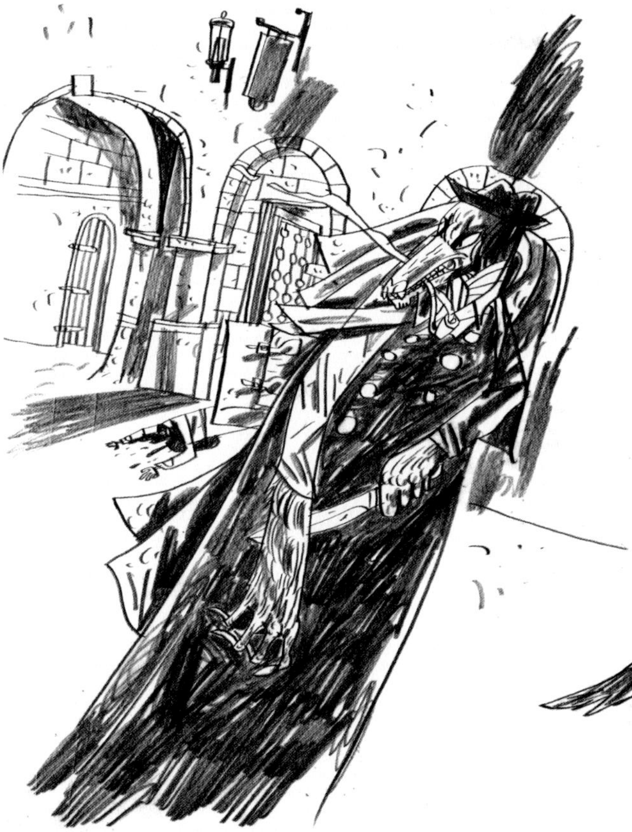

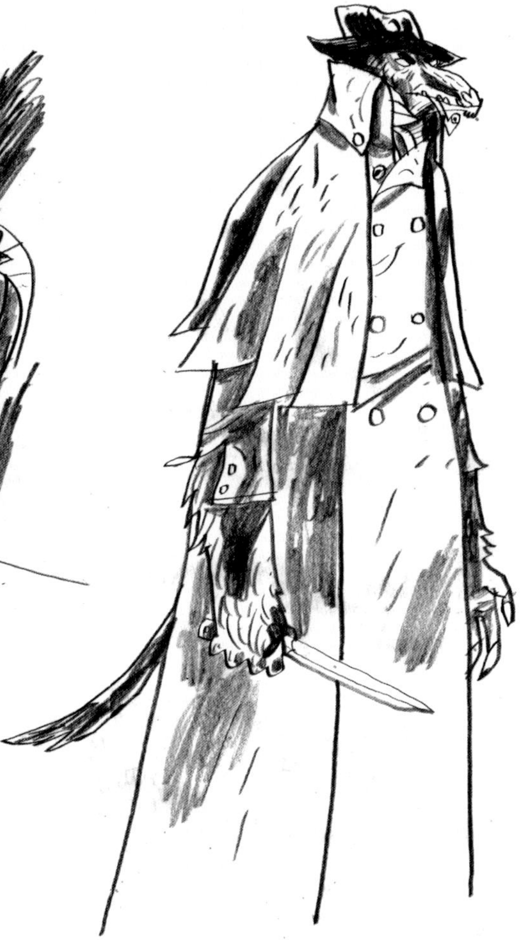

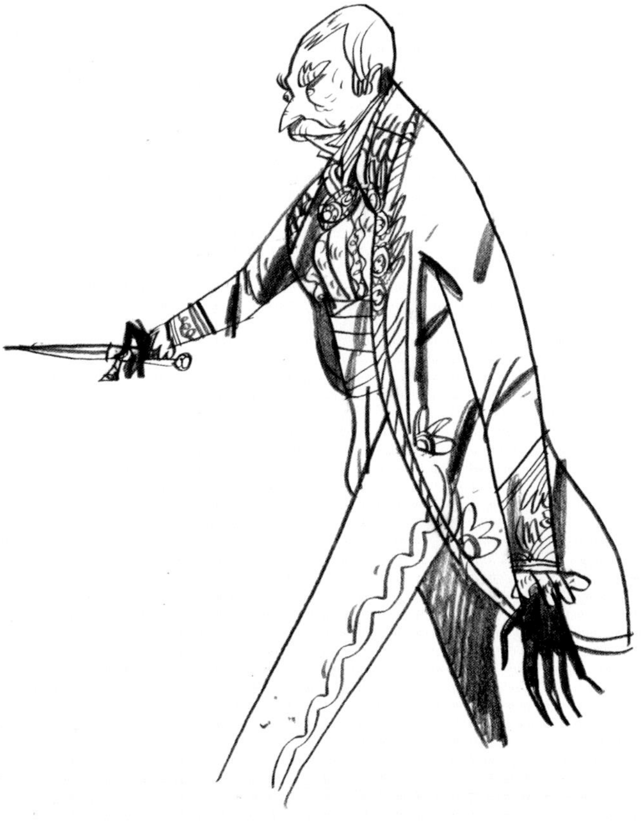

I was happy to return to this world and embrace the well-known elements of the classic horror tradition, but I did also want to add something different to the cauldron.

RECOMMENDED READING

MR. HIGGINS COMES HOME
Story by Mike Mignola
Art by Warwick Johnson-Cadwell
978-1-50670-466-1 • $14.99

HELLBOY IN HELL LIBRARY EDITION
Story and art by Mike Mignola
978-1-50670-363-3 • $49.99

HELLBOY: INTO THE SILENT SEA
Story by Mike Mignola and Gary Gianni
Art by Gary Gianni
978-1-50670-143-1 • $14.99

THE AMAZING SCREW-ON HEAD AND OTHER CURIOUS OBJECTS
Story and art by Mike Mignola
978-1-59582-501-8 • $17.99

THE DARK HORSE BOOK OF HORROR
Story and art by Mike Mignola and various
978-1-50670-372-5 • $19.99

THE SHAOLIN COWBOY: SHEMP BUFFET
Story and art by Geof Darrow
978-1-61655-726-3 • $19.99

BEASTS OF BURDEN: ANIMAL RITES
Story by Evan Dorkin
Art by Jill Thompson
978-1-59582-513-1 • $19.99

BAIT: OFF-COLOR STORIES FOR YOU TO COLOR
Stories by Chuck Palahniuk
978-1-50670-311-4 • $19.99

EDGAR ALLAN POE'S SPIRITS OF THE DEAD
Story and art by Richard Corben
978-1-61655-356-2 • $24.99

RAT GOD
Story and art by Richard Corben
978-1-61655-769-0 • $19.99

HARROW COUNTY VOLUME 1: COUNTLESS HAINTS
Story by Cullen Bunn
Art by Tyler Crook
978-1-61655-780-5 • $14.99

ALEISTER & ADOLF
Story by Douglas Rushkoff
Art by Michael Avon Oeming
978-1-50670-104-2 • $19.99

GARY GIANNI'S MONSTERMEN AND OTHER SCARY STORIES
Story and art by Gary Gianni
978-1-50670-480-7 • $19.99

THE SHADOW GLASS
Story and art by Aly Fell
978-1-50670-082-3 • $19.99

BERNIE WRIGHTSON'S FRANKENSTEIN
Story by Mary Wollstonecraft Shelley
Art by Bernie Wrightson
978-1-59582-200-0 • $34.99

DEAR CREATURE
Story and art by Jonathan Case
978-1-50670-095-3 • $22.99

BEDTIME GAMES
Story by Nick Keller
Art by Conor Nolan
978-1-50670-901-7 • $17.99

JENNY FINN
Story by Mike Mignola and Troy Nixey
Art by Troy Nixey and Farel Dalrymple
978-1-50670-544-6 • $17.99

SHADOWS ON THE GRAVE
Story and art by Richard Corben
978-1-50670-391-6 • $19.99

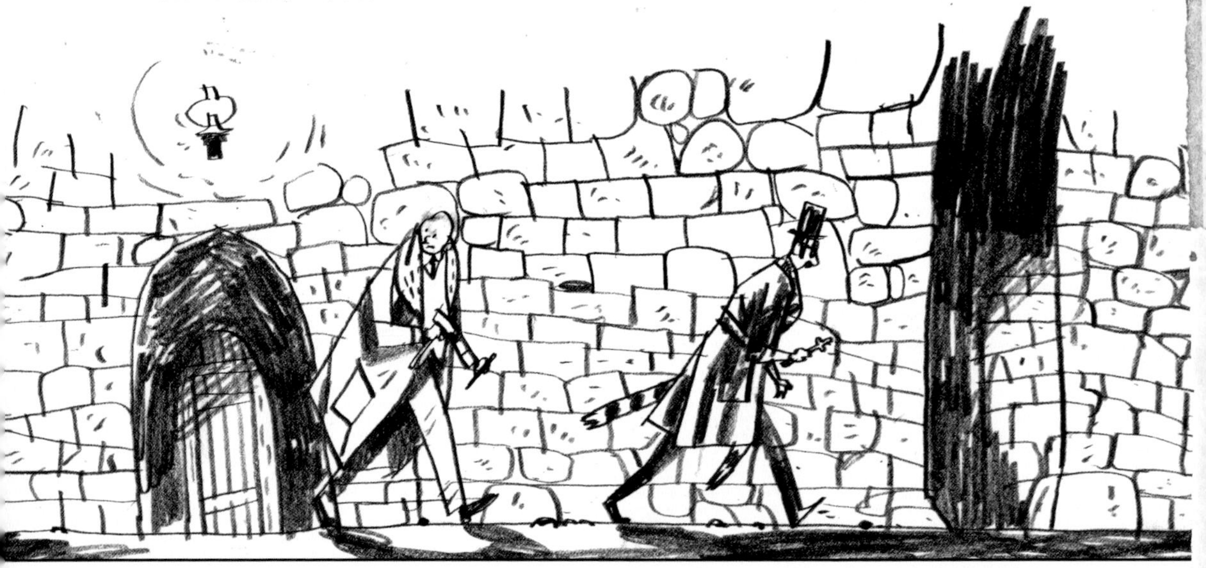